SUBDUCTION ZONE

By

COLIN SETTERFIELD

TABLE OF CONTENTS

One

Precursory Tremors.
Monday, 6:15 a.m. 18th September.

Paul Brinkworth sat on the balcony of the cottage, gazing across the Juan de Fuca Strait. He could barely see the distant snow-capped mountains partly shrouded in mist. The breeze ruffled his dark, wavy hair tousled from the night's sleep, and his features displayed pleasure as the early morning rays caressed his face.

It had been a restful weekend. Taking time off to spend two days in Sooke had been Megan's idea. Paul had been working long hours and the family needed more time together. He felt refreshed and ready for the week that lay ahead—the meetings with senior management, the pending trip to Tofino, and all the work involved in monitoring the instruments at the various seismic monitoring stations on the island. It was time to rouse everyone and return to the family home in nearby Victoria. In his preponderance he could almost feel the pre-weekend stress clutching for his mind.

A slight vibration ran through the building causing the balcony to sway imperceptibly; time appeared to stop for interminable seconds before the early morning sounds rushed back in symphonic concert—a moment that caught the attention of his finely honed senses. Paul appeared thoughtful as he stood gripping the balcony railing with both hands.

Grateful for the years of research, knowledge, and experience, he knew how to interpret recent events. Thoughts of the immediate future floated in his mind as he turned toward the sliding door leading to the bedroom.

"Honey, did you feel that tremor?"

No answer from the submerged form under the duvet as he rushed in to grab the cell phone next to the bed. He quickly keyed in the number and waited eagerly for his friend to answer.

"Hello, Tom? Did you feel that tremor a few moments ago?"

The dull tone of Tom's voice suggested he had been awakened from a deep sleep. Paul tore on regardless.

"I know it's very early to be calling, but we've just had another event. It lasted about eight seconds— that's three tremors in about nineteen days. Our theory appears to have some foundation."

The sleepy monotone changed to a series of startled grunts.

"I know you're not lecturing today, so let's take a trip up to Tofino and check on the instruments.

Since Fowler doesn't agree the subduction zone is on the move, I won't say anything to the rest of the staff. But I believe the readings on the instruments will show some interesting changes in elevation. Pick you up at eight-thirty?"

**

Monday, 6:18 a.m. 18th September.

Tom Wilson sat up in bed and rubbed sleep from his eyes. His boney fingers probed the wrinkles on his face as he stared at the opposite wall, attempting to focus on a framed family photo.

He and Paul Brinkworth went back a long way—to his final year on campus. Paul had been a freshman when they discovered they shared common interests in the sciences.

"What's happening, honey?" asked Gertrude, now awake and eyeing her husband through half-opened lids.

Tom hesitated at the bathroom door. "Umm... Paul and I are taking a trip to Tofino today. We need to check on some aspects of the work he's been doing there."

She disapproved of Paul Brinkworth. He always thought he was right about everything and had a habit of being short with her when she attempted to venture into their area of expertise. Seismology, the subject that Paul and Tom discussed at great length, was a topic of which she knew very little.

She'd never taken much interest in her husband's career. After all, that was his business. As long as he provided the things they needed as a family, she was content. The subject of geophysics was far too technical for her mind and the attempts she made to understand the jargon only confused her more.

"Why does he need you to go with him, love?" she asked.

"He needs to recalibrate some of the instruments and wants my opinion on something before he broaches the findings to his boss," Tom answered hesitantly.

"What time will you be back?"

"By nightfall. You didn't need me to do anything for you today, did you?"

"No—I'll be going to the ladies' meeting at the church and the kids need their usual rides to sporting activities."

"You sure it's okay?" asked Tom.

"Sure—do your thing with your seismological sidekick but don't be late for dinner because I've invited Ian and Georgia Hamilton."

Tom grunted an acknowledgment as he moved into the bathroom, eager to escape his wife's piercing glare.

Why the Hamiltons for goodness sake?   He disrobed and stepped into the shower. The warm water flowed over his bony chest and down his spidery legs. He usually struggled to relate to Gertrude's friends. She knew he didn't like Ian Hamilton.

Tom toweled himself off and then started shaving as Gertrude entered the shower.

"Did you hear what I said about the Hamiltons, honey?"

"I did respond," he said gruffly.

"But you didn't seem happy."

"You know how I struggle to make conversation with Ian."

"I know, but it's important to me, honey—he's an elder in the church."

"He's still a bore! And Georgia speaks so quickly— I struggle to understand what she says."

"She just gets excited, sweetheart."

"I get the impression they want to convert me."

"They mean well, honey."

Tom looked at his watch. "I should get dressed."

**

Monday, 2:00 p.m. 18th September.

After three and a half hours of driving, Paul and Tom arrived at their destination. The preamble to the small village of Tofino featured a rainforest, a popular area where summer tourists could venture into tall trees and lush vegetation and view a variety of flora.

The National Parks Department had granted permission to establish a temporary seismological station to monitor land movement but many saw it as an intrusion into nature and were openly opposed to it.

Paul turned off the highway into the visitor's area and found a spot to leave the Jeep. He made sure the official permit was placed on top of the dash and they headed for the rainforest trail. Out of the corner of his eye, Paul noticed two people climb out of a truck near the permit dispenser.

*

"Well, everything seems to be all right here," Paul noted as they looked around the monitoring site for anything that might be missing, or out of place.

Tom gazed around the small site and nodded in agreement. A sudden rustling of bushes nearby made the two men glance up. They looked into the piercing eyes of a man who appeared to be in his early thirties—the individual was clean-shaven and wore a tweed jacket. His hair, parted down the middle and sporting long sideburns, depicted a distinctive "sixties" look. Perspiration glistened on his brow.

For a long moment they stared at one another. "What the freakin' hell are you doing here? Did you wander off the boardwalk and get lost? You need a permit to be in this area," Paul blurted.

A young woman came from behind the man and stood next to him, arms folded defiantly and glared at Paul. She was a plain, earthy woman with dark-brown hair and green eyes. The blue windbreaker she wore was oversized and the tightly fitting blue jeans flaunted her well-formed thighs and calves.

"My name's Sean O'Kelly." The man spoke with a strong Irish brogue and a calm, self-assured tone of voice. "We're with an environmental consciousness group and we've come to the park several times now, hoping to see someone from the Geological Survey Centre—reckon today we finally got lucky."

For a moment Paul was speechless, but quickly regained his composure and stepped forward assertively.

"We have the permission of the Park Board to be here, which is more than I can say for you—so if you think you can intimidate us with your green consciousness nonsense, then you're mistaken."

The woman interjected, her hard eyes staring unblinkingly at Paul. "I don't think it would do us any good to get into a shouting match. All we want is for you to hear us out and then we'll be on our way."

Without giving Paul or Tom a chance to object, she launched into a mission speech.

"We are custodians of the environment. How in God's name do you think the forest is going to survive if people like you are constantly tampering with it?"

"We're not tampering with the environment," Paul answered.

The woman was not deterred. "Don't you realize how sensitive this ecological system is? Our being here, walking, breathing, talking and littering is striking at the forest's heart. You have cleared away important undergrowth and disturbed the forest floor with your confounded platform."

Tom responded, pointing to the equipment. "I think you guys have taken this thing about the environment too far. These instruments constitute a very important warning device. We are scientists and we know what we are doing. We have had the local branch of the National Park authority to advise and help us. This monitoring station is the very thing that could save lives in the future by warning us as to what's taking place beneath the surface of the ground."

"We don't give a damn about your experiments, or what's beneath the ground," responded the Irishman. "We say Mother Nature has her own way of sorting things out if we let her. Several letters have been sent to the Minister of the Environment

11

and she's just ignored us! We've also sent letters to the center, but you've also chosen to ignore us, so you know what the next step is going to be, don't you?"

Paul became heated. "Don't you even consider touching this equipment. We'll go straight to the R.C.M.P. if you so much as threaten us!"

The woman turned to O'Kelly with a gesture of her hand. "Let's go, Sean. Let's get outta here."

O'Kelly turned to follow her and then hesitated. Turning again to the two perplexed scientists he said: "Gentlemen, as Hilda mentioned in the beginning, it'll not serve any purpose to argue. I want to leave you with this ultimatum—either this station of yours is removed within one week, or we take it out ourselves. Now you can call the cops if you want, but you can't guard this facility night and day. Eventually we will win. We always do."

With that they turned and delicately worked their way through the foliage in the direction of the boardwalk.

Paul and Tom stood gaping with their hands on their hips, trying to assimilate what just transpired.

"Well, what do you make of that?" asked Tom. "Do you think they meant what they said?"

Paul scratched his chin and stared in the direction of the departing environmentalists.

"Hard to say. It's difficult to believe that people can take such a strong stand against something that's there to protect them—I wouldn't discount it though."

"What do you think we should do?" A worried frown creased Tom's brow as he looked at the monitoring site.

"Nothing, for the moment. I will record it in my log and also mention it to Fowler when I return to the center. We'll have to wait and see. After all, the Irishman was right—we don't have the resources to institute fulltime surveillance."

"I've heard about environmentalists who spike trees with metal in order to frustrate the loggers. Do you think they could sabotage these instruments in such a way that might be dangerous?"

"Anything's possible. I don't see how we can adequately protect the site without bringing harm to the flora. It was quite a task to obtain the park's authority for what we have here at the moment," Paul said. "It's almost impossible to keep out the determined thief."

"How important is this particular site? Couldn't we establish a new one close by, on the fringe of the forest? Does it have to be right here?"

"Our surveys show this will be the exact area where the maximum change in elevation will take place. I'm not about to be defeated by a group of hard-nosed individuals who have no appreciation for their own safety."

Paul sighed as he moved towards the instruments. Muttering under his breath, he knelt with both hands on the platform for support, and lowered his head into the observation hole to peer at the equipment. The readings were transmitted automatically by satellite to the survey center but a small gauge was provided for onsite monitoring.

The light was beginning to fail so he tried to bring his face as close to the instrument as possible in order to read the measurement. Tom was about to comment when Paul let out a low whistle.

"Tom! Take a look at this!

**

Monday, 3:15 p.m. 18th September.

By three o'clock that afternoon, Megan Brinkworth was almost finished with the family laundry. She had spent the morning cleaning the house, a chore she never enjoyed.

The children were enough work for ten mothers and she was constantly pitting her wits against her twelve-year-old son's relentless testing of her authority and resolve.

Jason would listen to his father without a murmur, but whenever Paul was away, the boy did not see the need to obey anyone. Meg had often mentioned Jason's behavior but Paul shrugged it off as a phase.

Their daughter, Amy, on the other hand, was very mature at fourteen and gave her parents little trouble. Her feisty nature was tempered with good humor and most of the time she was a delight to have around. The squabbles between her and Jason usually ended with both of them being sent off to their respective bedrooms.

Megan's thoughts were interrupted as the front door burst open and Jason stormed in like a wounded buffalo, flinging his school bag onto the floor.

"Mom? I'm dying of hunger. I've eaten nothing since breakfast—I forgot to take my lunch money... what can I eat?"

"If you're that hungry, help yourself to some bread, and don't drink all the milk," Megan answered in exasperation.

"But I'm thirsty!"

"Your father will want his coffee when he gets home and we need to keep enough for breakfast tomorrow."

She continued folding clothes, bending down every now and then to extricate more from the drier.

Once again the door opened and Amy, slightly flushed by the brisk walk from the bus stop, entered. She strode to the living room, ignoring her brother, who was peering into all the kitchen cupboards, and said, "Hi, Mom. Guess what? I got an A plus for that English essay I wrote last week."

"That's wonderful, darling. Which essay was it?"

"The one on earthquake-prone areas. I wrote what Dad told me about the Pacific Rim and the huge Alaskan earthquake in 1964. It sure pays to have a seismologist for a father."

"I'm sure Dad will be very proud of you and that you take such an interest in what he does. If you're not careful he'll have you working for him."

Jason stuck his head around the corner and added sarcastically: "She's too useless to be of any help to Dad—she's just sucking up so she can go out with those stupid friends of hers on Saturday night."

Amy rounded on him. "Shut up, Jason. You don't know what you're talking about. You're only twelve and you don't even have hair on your legs yet, so get outta my face! In fact, get outta my life!"

"Jason! Amy! Stop your fighting. Can't either of you ever say a kind word to one another?"

The siblings glared at each other and then turned to look at her questioningly. Jason feigned surprise and then stuck his tongue out at his sister.

Meg looked at each child in turn. A wisp of hair hung down, tickling her nose. She flicked it away irritably and was dismayed to find tears stinging her eyes. *No, Meg, don't cry in front of them. That won't help!* She composed herself and carried on with her chores.

"My goodness, what would your father say if he could hear the two of you going at each other? Go upstairs, both of you, and get changed. Your grandmother is coming at four this afternoon to visit."

∞

Two

The Geological Survey Center: Dept. of Seismic Studies.

Tuesday, 9:00 a.m. 19th September.

Paul entered through the glass doors marked "Geological Survey Centre" and strode down the carpeted hallway to his office. The GSC was the section dealing with seismic activities in the Pacific region and served jointly with the Institute of Ocean Sciences.

Margaret, the division secretary, was filing and the solemn look on her face indicated the atmosphere in the building was tense. Paul instinctively knew that John Fowler, his immediate superior, had been finding fault again.

Margaret turned when she heard Paul's rap on the counter. "Oh, it's you!" She straightened and smiled.

"You've certainly disturbed a hornet's nest."

"I thought my discovery would get management's attention. What did Fowler say?" Paul asked.

She placed hands on her hips. "The usual."

"He doesn't agree there could be a problem?"

Margaret made a face. "Well, he didn't exactly say."

"What did he say?"

"Nothing—just shook his head."

Paul smiled wryly. "By the atmosphere in the building, I guess he's in his office."

"Yes, he's been talking to the heads of the other departments. He's been telling them you are trying to draw a conclusion from data that might not be directly related to an earthquake."

"You mean he doesn't believe we have possible tectonic plate immobility?"

Margaret made a gesture of dismissal with her hand. "You know how obnoxious he is—he has never agreed to the plates being completely immobile in the first place."

"As always, he is misquoting me," said Paul.

Margaret sat at her desk. "The director wants you in his office right away—he wants to discuss your theory along with other departmental issues."

"Is everyone included?"

She nodded. "John's already there."

Paul headed for his office to get his notebook.

When he arrived at the director's office, the door was closed and the others were standing in the hallway chatting. Fowler was not amongst them.

The head of the Marine Geological subdivision greeted him. Another seismologist working mostly with the North Island Survey was also there.

Paul knocked on the director's door.

"Come in, it's open."

Paul entered with the other two men and couldn't help noticing the scowl on Fowler's face.

The director and Fowler had obviously been discussing the issue and Fowler would have already added his negative remarks regarding Paul's theory.

The director stood and shifted the scattered papers on his desk to one side as the others took seats around his desk.

His boss gave Paul a disapproving glance. Their relationship was generally one of cool tolerance, but of late, it appeared that Fowler was threatened by Paul's involvement in the recent monitoring activities.

As head of Seismic Studies, John Fowler considered it beneath his station to go into the field. He believed himself to be the only person with an informed opinion on Vancouver Island's seismic activities.

The director dropped his chin and peered over the top of his spectacles at each man in turn.

Dark rings hung under his eyes, and his usual jovial demeanor was absent.

"Gentlemen, thank you for coming so promptly. I won't keep you long because I realize you're all busy. The news that Paul phoned through yesterday has everybody speculating and we need to satisfy ourselves as to the magnitude of the problem before the press gets onto it."

The director leaned forward, focusing his attention on Paul.

"Now, what reports have you had from the stations around the Tofino area?"

"All the stations record a similar rise in elevation. The trilateration survey shows some changes in horizontal distances between the various survey monuments. There is also a definite change in crust density in the general Tofino, Ucluelet area."

"Do you think the plates are separating?" the director asked.

"Yes. It's inevitable, if the pressure continues to build at the present rate."

Fowler scowled and interjected, "I'm sure there's no reason for any real concern. The island has shown significant increases in elevation before— without an earthquake."

Paul was not going to allow John to play down the danger. "It's not just the fact we've had a few tremors. It's the diminishing time intervals between them."

He and John often clashed over the interpretation of seismic event causes and conclusions. John's shoulders bristled and he glared at Paul.

"We can't tell the public an earthquake is imminent. There will be a mass panic!"

Paul shook his head and said nothing.

The others were silent, their eyes on John and Paul. The director softened his tone. "John, nobody is going to start a panic, but we need to be prepared for the worst. Paul, what do you think the tremors signify?"

Paul paused for a moment. "This is just a hunch." Here was his opportunity to press home his theory. Or was it to silence Fowler? "The focal points of the tremors appear to be in the general Tofino, Ucluelet area. The diminishing frequencies of their occurrences are enough to start me thinking seriously about the Big One. We can all appreciate that when pre-quake tremors, in a subduction zone, have decreasing intervals of occurrence, it indicates a clear and present danger that the plates are breaking free."

Interested expressions on the faces of his colleagues eased his anxiety about his theory. The director paled slightly, but John's face remained expressionless.

Paul stood and placed his hands on the director's desk. The men were hanging on every word. He paused in a mixture of fear and excitement.

"I believe the Juan de Fuca plate is beginning to move. These decreasing interval events we are now experiencing are the possible precursor to a very sudden separation of the Juan de Fuca and North American plates. When that happens we will have the makings of a major catastrophe on our hands."

John shifted uncomfortably in his seat and tapped his pencil annoyingly on the polished desktop. Paul felt his antagonism but continued regardless. "We could be in for a megathrust."

The room was silent as they assimilated what Paul said. John didn't offer any resistance to Paul's theory. He smiled wryly indicating his thoughts on the speculations.

The head of the Marine Geological division sitting opposite the desk from Paul leaned forward.

"There has been movement on the continental slope. This could verify what Paul is saying. I know nobody can predict an earthquake scientifically, but there is definitely some merit in his theory. I think we should wait a few more days and see what develops before talking to the press."

The other seismologist nodded.

John squirmed lower in his seat and stared out the window as though something outside was far more interesting.

The director concurred: "That seems to be good strategy but we need to keep a lid on it—should the press contact any of you, keep a low profile. You can say we'll know more in a few days. It goes without saying the island's inhabitants should make sure they are well prepared for a seismic event. Agreed, gentlemen?"

All nodded except Fowler, who glared at the ceiling.

Paul left the director's office and walked down a flight of stairs to his own office on the main floor. He noticed that John stayed on to talk with the director.

A postmortem, no doubt, he thought as he turned left into the corridor that led to their division. He glanced at his wristwatch—almost time for a coffee break and a good opportunity to think about what he would say if the press called.

As Paul passed Margaret's office, she called to him. "Someone to see you, Paul—a lady from the press. Says she only wants to talk to you and not to John. She's waiting in your office—nice looking girl." Margaret wagged a finger at him. "I'll have to keep an eye on you two. She's far too gorgeous to be left alone with you."

"Oh, come on, Margaret—don't exaggerate," Paul said, annoyed that he would be deemed susceptible.

"Wait until you see her," answered Margaret with a knowing smile.

"Did she make an appointment?" Paul asked, trying to appear uninterested.

"No, but she said her schedule was extremely tight and would be grateful if you could give her a few minutes of your time."

"You should have told her to come back on another day. I have things to do."

"I thought you would want to get it over with—anyway, she's waiting in your office."

Paul closed his eyes and shook his head. *The press descending already? Why him?* He strode to his office, apprehensive of the pending interview. The lady may be pretty but she was still a reporter.

He stopped outside the door to smooth down his hair and check his breath. Normal protocol would be to hand it off to Fowler but just the thought of the man regurgitating seismic drivel with his normal self-elevating attitude persuaded Paul to do the interview himself. Then he stepped into the office.

When he saw the reporter, he understood what Margaret meant. The lady was standing with her back to him, admiring a painting on the wall. On hearing him enter the room she turned and he was immediately taken with her beauty. Long blond hair cascaded loosely onto her shoulders and flowed down her back, reflecting sparkling highlights from the overhead fluorescent.

She stood poised, like a professional model, posing for a photo shoot. Paul was conscious of holding his breath and immediately felt annoyed because he knew it showed. He felt a warm glow spreading over his face.

"Oh, hi—I'm Paul," he stammered and stretched out his hand, knowing she was sizing him up.

"Hi, Paul, my name's Angeline Summers."

Her husky voice caressed his hearing like a warm breeze on a balmy morning. He smelled the sultry fragrance of her perfume and it sent his pulse racing.

"I was in Sidney earlier this morning when my boss asked if I would call in on you. I believe you know him? Andrew Mortimer?"

Paul hesitated and with some difficulty tried to coax his breathing back to its normal rhythm. "Yes, of course. We play golf together occasionally. Please sit and make yourself comfortable. What can I do for you?" He tried to stop himself from staring at her like a horny teenager.

"Andrew asked me to speak to you. He said you'd be straight with me. He got a call from a Mr. O'Kelly who is apparently involved in some sort of conservation movement."

Paul's infatuation with Miss Summers suddenly evaporated and his focus zoomed back to planet Earth. He waited.

"Did you have a confrontation with this person in the rainforest?"

Paul shrugged.

"Who is this O'Kelly person?"

Paul shrugged again. "A guy who works for one of the environmentalist groups, I guess."

"Was he alone?"

"There was a woman."

"Did this have anything to do with the monitoring station?"

Paul again hesitated but this time not from enchantment. He realized the need to be careful and not give anything away regarding the tremors. "They felt we were endangering the environment."

"Why put a seismic station in the rainforest?"

Paul leaned forward and spoke with caution. "It has been necessary, from a ground monitoring point of view. That is the only comment I can make as to the reason for it being there."

"But surely there are other areas it could be placed?"

He looked out the window as he considered the question. Then after a brief moment he turned to face her again. "It's always necessary to put a site where the most accurate measurements can be taken."

She smiled, finding his evasiveness amusing.

"I heard rumors of an impending quake involving tectonic plate movement. Is that the reason why you are monitoring in this particular place?"

Paul knew they were getting into forbidden territory. His mind grasped furiously for some way to change the subject.

"The Pacific Rim has always been a sensitive seismic area. The possibility of tremor activity morphing into an earthquake has always been a part of what we live with..."

He knew his reluctance to deal with the questions was showing.

Angeline tilted her head and raised her eyebrows. "But do you think the tremors have a connection to that area? Are they not perhaps leading up to something bigger? Is there a possibility that the long expected Big One is about to happen?"

This was the question Paul had been dreading. He tried to play it down.

"People are always speculating, but I assure you there is no scientific way to predict an earthquake. Its common knowledge the island is accumulating strain due to the potential of locked crustal plates. We are monitoring the situation. When we have anything to report we will. And now, Ms. Summers, we have to be responsible stewards of the knowledge that comes to us—we don't want to cause any undue panic."

He became aware that beads of perspiration were accumulating on his brow.

"Please call me Angeline. Is it not responsible to publish all the findings on a daily basis and allow the people to decide themselves?" she offered calmly.

"Yes and no. We have to be absolutely sure what we tell them is not based purely on speculation."

At that moment Paul glanced at the office door and saw John Fowler standing there, obviously waiting to be introduced.

"Please meet the department chief, John Fowler."

He couldn't help feeling a measure of scorn as John overdid his grin and shook her hand vigorously, staring into her eye's like a snake about to strike its victim.

"And what brings such a lovely young lady to our part of the world?" he gurgled, totally enamored with Angeline's good looks.

Paul quickly answered before Angeline could say anything.

"Miss Summers is from the press. She has an interest in the monitoring site at Tofino."

John did not take his eyes off her. Putting on his most charming smile he asked: "Is there anything I can help you with?"

Angeline answered before Paul could.

"Not really. I thought it would be good for me to have a look at the center and learn a little about the seismic monitoring process."

John ignored Paul's stern glare and rambled on. "I'm sure with my long experience here at the center I would be able to deepen your interest in the wonderful subject of seismology. I've virtually grown up with a seismometer in my hand."

"If I feel I need more information, you will be the next person I will ask," she said reassuringly.

John looked peeved and let go of her hand. He turned to Paul and said: "Don't forget to bring the results of the most recent surveys to me. I need to check your calculations."

He turned back to Angeline and said, "You are welcome to visit us—make sure you ask for me at the front desk if you come again. I know more about this business than anyone else and I will definitely be able to answer all your questions."

Angeline nodded and gave Fowler a dismissive smile. Paul was furious at the intrusion and was determined to get Fowler out of his office. Deciding that further conversation would be counterproductive Paul intimated that he had things to do and suggested that Angeline come at another time when he would be able to show her around the center.

She picked up her purse and cell phone.

"I look forward to meeting with you again and I'll definitely hold you to your suggestion. It would be great to check out the whole establishment. Thank you for your time, Paul."

"I will see you to your car," Paul said, ignoring Fowler completely. They left him standing, ogling her shapely behind as they exited the office and walked down the corridor.

In the entrance foyer, hanging on the wall, was a beautifully illustrated diagram in cross-section describing how earthquakes are caused and how fault lines deep within the earth relieve the buildup of subterranean pressures. Angeline stopped to look up at the diagram and turned to Paul.

"This diagram is very well done—it's hard to believe we could be facing an earthquake in the near future."

Paul glanced at the diagram. "You mean the long awaited Big One?"

She nodded.

"Time will tell," answered Paul, conscious that she was looking deeply into his eyes.

"Don't forget that invitation to see the facility."

"I won't," he said. "Just let me know when you can come again."

They stood looking at each other for a few seconds then she smiled and stuck out her hand as he opened one of the double glass doors. He felt her soft, delicate hand engulfed by his own larger, rough-skinned fingers and his heart skipped a beat as he sensed a primal urge to take her in his arms.

The handshake was a suitable gesture, but both seemed reluctant to release their grip. Finally he let go of her hand and she walked toward the car, looking back once waving a final goodbye. He watched her get into her vehicle before heading back to his office.

A glimmer of guilt nibbled at his soul—the thought of how easily Angeline had stirred him. She was a person of danger but also a person of great interest. A bivalent conflict reared up in his mind. The press, at this time, was to be seen as a danger, but Angeline was different. Not only was she extremely attractive but intelligent and interesting. He did not think she posed any threat to the center's need for confidentiality—but then one could never be sure with the press.

Margaret was waiting for him. "Well, how did your interview go? Did she get you going?"

"Not really."

"You didn't find her attractive?"

"Of course I found her attractive; what man wouldn't?"

"Don't get defensive. I was just asking. John wants to talk to you."

Paul sighed and went into his office. He had promised to give Tom a call after the meeting with the GSC management. His thoughts ranged back to Angeline. He could still smell the fragrance of her perfume in his office—still see her beautiful face, with those sensual lips, parted in a glimmer of a smile. He knew he wanted to see her again.

∞

Three

Discussing Paul's Theory.
Tuesday, 2:00 p.m. 19th September.

Paul placed the call to Tom's office hoping to catch his friend between lectures. Tom answered immediately. Paul quickly launched into his theory again. "We've experienced several significant tremors to date. The last tremor was at 6:30 a.m. Monday the 18th. My records show we've had three tremors over approximately nineteen days, each event diminishing by almost half the time of its predecessor!"

Tom was silent for a moment, quickly doing a calculation in his mind. "That would give us approximately three to four days before the plates break free from one another—if your theory is correct. You certainly seem to be onto something. We need to check the instruments again and make a specific chart of the events with their time separations and magnitudes. How does the director feel about your theory?"

"I don't think he takes it very seriously but he is cautious enough not to discount it." Paul rubbed his chin. "John Fowler would have given him all sorts of reasons to doubt me, but even he will have to take notice of the deliberate progression of the tremors."

Paul had already charted the events with all relevant information. He speculated that if the theory was correct, then the next tremor would be in two days, followed by another, a day later.

"I don't think in terms of speculation anymore," Tom stated. "The question in my mind is what to do. Should we take our families and leave on a short vacation, or do we stay and see what transpires?"

Paul shifted in his seat. "There's no telling what magnitude the quake will be. I'm confident we have enough emergency measures in place to handle a magnitude seven but what if something bigger comes along?"

"I'm worried about the attitude of the people—when they read the latest reports. I can imagine a stampede to the airport," said Tom.

"I'm not so sure," Paul responded. "The islanders are pretty laid back. They have repeatedly been warned about the possibilities. I think fatalism will probably prevail."

Tom shrugged. "Of particular concern to me is the possibility of a tsunami hitting the west coast. Tofino, Ucluelet and Port Alberni will definitely be at risk."

"Yeah, the '64 Alaskan quake caused a lot of damage. There are many more people in these towns—more buildings on the waterfront."

"But are you aiming to stay on the island or take a sudden vacation?" Tom asked.

"I want to be here if it happens. No vacations for me just yet," stated Paul emphatically.

He felt more would be achieved by staying to monitor the preamble and then helping with the ensuing emergency situation and clean up that would follow.

After they had discussed the matter at length, the two men ended their conversation with the thought of meeting for a game of golf on the weekend.

Paul returned his attention to perusing the latest seismographic records.

There was a knock on the door jamb. He looked up to see the director standing there. "Paul? I heard you had a visitor from the press."

Paul was immediately on guard. "Yeah, she asked some pertinent questions."

"We really need to be careful at this stage. Was it due to the tremors that her interest in a possible earthquake was aroused?"

"Not actually ..."

Paul went on to relate the details of O'Kelly's phone call to Andrew Mortimer, editor of the Victoria Herald.

"The press won't give up, so do your best to keep a lid on things." The director left with a nod.

Paul sat motionless for a while, a myriad of emotions swirling through his mind. His thoughts were initially for his family but finally rested on Angeline Summers. He wondered what she would do—if there were someone in her life who could help her in the event of a disaster.

He fantasized a little on the idea of rescuing her from the rubble of some building and reveling in her gratefulness while he gallantly carried her to safety. Suddenly the image of a tearful Megan floated into his mind and he realized, with a twinge of guilt, he was allowing his feelings to roam.

This was not like him. He loved his wife and children and would never wish to do anything to harm the relationship. Yet his thoughts kept returning to the fantasy image of a frightened, but grateful Angeline, clinging to him for comfort in the aftermath of a disaster.

Instinctively he realized he would have to be careful when they met again. It would not be expedient to give any clue of his feelings for her. At that moment Margaret walked into the office with the previous day's routine synopsis of seismometer results.

"Here are the reports. I'll have an analysis of yesterday's tremor from all the stations up north within thirty minutes—that woman from the press called while you were busy with the director."

Paul caught the emphasis that Margaret placed on that woman and shifted uneasily in his chair.

Margaret plowed on, "She wanted to know if you could arrange a tour of the facility for her as you promised. Did you really promise her that or was she just saying it to get around me?"

Paul felt a blush coming on and tried to control his emotions. Margaret obviously suspected something. The young lady was attractive and apparently single, a fact the receptionist had already assumed.

He cleared his throat and thanked Margaret, adding, "I just said it on the spur of the moment to needle John. He had come into my office and was boring her with his huge ego."

He was conscious that his cheeks were glowing and that he was scratching for excuses.

"I wouldn't wish to inflict Fowler's ego on anyone —to offer her a tour on another day seemed appropriate under the circumstance—she was beginning to ask difficult questions."

Margaret gave Paul her most knowing glare, supported by a smile to reinforce the message—she knew exactly what this young newspaper hussy was up to. No amount of covering by him could hide the truth. She turned on her heel and left the room with her nose in the air.

Paul shook his head and opened his desk diary to schedule a trip to Tofino for the next day. When he had scribbled in the note, he leaned back in his chair, deep in thought as he contemplated what he would say to Angeline. Then, dialing Margaret's number, he assumed a business-like tone. "Margaret, please get me the young journalist lady. I believe you have her cell number? Thank you."

Conscious of the fact he was perspiring slightly, he considered another meeting with Angeline, wondering how he would deal with her questions concerning the possibility of the earthquake.

He didn't know anything about her. He was not sure if he could trust her with any measure of confidentiality—or was she one of those fanatical newspaper people who habitually gleaned and published everything at any cost?

The ringing of the phone on his desk interrupted his contemplation. Nervously he picked up the receiver making a conscious effort to relax. Angeline's voice came on the line.

"Hi, Paul—I'm so glad you called me back. I was afraid you'd be reluctant to speak to anyone from the press again. Everyone's talking about the tremors and I really need to discuss it at greater length with you. I was hoping you would make good on the offer to tour the facility—then we could talk about the tremors at the same time."

Paul felt suddenly at ease, placated by her friendly tone and direct approach. Leaning over, he could see through the open door of his office. Margaret's stony glare met his quick glance. He winked at her and straightened in his chair.

"May I ask you a personal question, Angeline? Do you report everything you hear, or do you sometimes keep things off the record?"

There was a hesitation. "I usually let my editor decide if something is really confidential, but if you're prepared to tell me something that needs to be off the record, then I won't mention it in

my report—as long as it will lead to something that's newsworthy later."

Paul felt he had launched himself over a precipice with his next words. "Good. I'll meet you here Friday at 8:00 a.m. You can see the center and we'll discuss the situation, but I'm holding you to what you've just said."

"I'm always true to my word, Paul. I really hope you'll give me the opportunity to prove that in the future and thank you so much for seeing me."

"You're most welcome. I look forward to Friday. It's been a while since I showed anyone the facility and I hope you'll enjoy it."

"I second that," she replied and said goodbye.

Angeline's words would remain with him for the rest of the afternoon.

**

Late Tuesday Afternoon, 19th September.

Paul arrived home at 5:30 p.m. and parked his Jeep in the garage. Lengthening shadows, cast by the late afternoon sun shining through the maple trees, crept across the front lawn, dispelling the last remnants of daylight.

Meg was waiting at the front door to greet her husband.

"Hi, honey," she said wrapping her arms around him. "How were things at the office today?"

Paul responded, drawing her close, "I had a good day for once—Fowler was his obnoxious self as usual but I don't let it bother me anymore?"

Meg nodded, looking expectantly at her husband, knowing he wanted to tell her something.

Paul released her from the embrace. "I need to talk to you about what I suspect the cause of the tremors is, but please don't tell the kids—it's still speculative."

She enjoyed moments when her husband confided confidential information and was all ears to hear what he had to say.

He explained his theory of how the diminishing time differences between the tremors could be leading up to the tectonic plates breaking free from one another. A look of deep concern came over Meg's face as she looked into his eyes, her mind trying to grasp the enormity of what he was saying.

"What about our safety? Shouldn't we be making plans to evacuate the island? When do you expect the quake to take place?"

"I can't say for sure, honey, but I'll probably know more in the next two days or so. We can't just leave though. I feel people have enough emergency education to cope with an earthquake, provided it's not above eight on the Richter scale, but there's no telling how big it will be. Let's just sleep on it until the next tremor hits."

Paul explained that the press had got wind of the findings at Tofino. "I'm trying desperately not to give anything away as it's still only a theory."

Meg was suddenly reminded that the phone's voicemail had been activated. "Someone phoned while I was out shopping and left a message on the answering service. I didn't recognize the voice but all he said was that you needed to check on your instruments at Tofino."

Paul quickly checked the voicemail, playing back the only message of the day. He didn't recognize the voice which caused a worried frown to crease his forehead. He listened to the message several times.

"It's time for me to make the rounds to all the instruments up north again. I've actually arranged to go up to Tofino tomorrow morning. I'm not sure I'll be able to visit all of them but I definitely need to get to the one in the rainforest."

"I wonder who this mysterious caller is. You'd better be careful when you're up there," Meg said.

**

41

Wednesday, 7:30 a.m. 20th September.

Paul woke early the next morning to the chimes of his bedside alarm. Meg had already risen so the household would have an early start.

He showered, dressed, and descended to the kitchen where a hearty breakfast of bacon and eggs awaited him. Ten minutes later he said goodbye to his family.

It was cloudy for most of the journey but after cresting the mountains before Ucluelet, the sun made its appearance. Four hours after leaving Victoria, he drove into the parking lot at the rainforest.

It took him thirty minutes to reach the monitoring site, his left leg hurting as it often did when he jogged or took a brisk walk. The old injury was the result of boarding during a hockey game back in the days when he played for the Victoria Cougars.

The platform was covered by a tarpaulin tied to the four corner posts of the platform. Paul untied the knots and yanked the tarp to one side.

As he was in a kneeling position to look at the seismometer, the ground shook slightly. Another tremor—a total of four tremors since they started on the 29th of August.

He looked at his watch—12:10 p.m. He peered at the seismometer for a reading, but found he was looking at an empty base. The instrument had been removed, leaving a gaping hole in its place.

"Damn it! Those environmental bastards have been here!" Paul cursed the Irishman and his female accomplice until he ran out of breath. He was sitting on his haunches on the platform when there was a soft rustling of leaves behind him.

He turned and caught a fleeting glimpse of a quick movement. A second later an excruciating pain exploded on the back of his head.

He tried to roll but was not quick enough as a man wearing a black ski mask bowled him over. The pain in his head increased dramatically and blood spouted from the inch long wound on his cranium. Strength began to ebb from his muscles as he struggled to remain conscious.

The attacker, aided mostly by the element of surprise, quickly gained the upper hand. Paul finally released his grip, slumping onto his side, with the man straddling him. The last thing he remembered was the stale smell of the man's clothing.

Sean O'Kelly silently appeared out of the surrounding forest carrying a box which he placed on the ground. His accomplice, Andre Banville, dragged Paul off the platform and tied his hands behind his back with a rope. Banville opened the

43

cardboard box to remove the seismometer extricated the previous day from the monitoring platform and tied it to Paul's limp body.

O'Kelly pulled a syringe from his pocket and pulled up the sleeve of Paul's jacket. He deftly pushed the plunger to dismiss air from the needle and expertly thrust the needle into Paul's forearm.

"That will put him out for at least fifteen hours. Go back to the lab and bring the first aid kit. We'll have to bandage up this wound on his head or he'll die from loss of blood."

He took out a handkerchief and placed it on the cut on Paul's head in an attempt to stem the blood flow. "Better hurry. I'll try to keep the wound closed."

"I guess I hit him a little too hard," Banville growled.

O'Kelly glanced at his accomplice. "Yeah—we need to be careful. Rushmore won't like it if we deal with too harsh a hand at this stage."

Andre smirked and said, "That surprises me—the great Barry Rushmore, dealing with a soft touch. He's a hard-ass."

O'Kelly shrugged. "He's the boss—we do as he says."

Andre jumped up and made his way through the forest undergrowth. In ten minutes he returned with a small first aid kit, folded stretcher, and a blanket with which they covered Paul. Then both settled down to wait for the next step.

By the time darkness fell, it was almost seven p.m. The two men gingerly lifted the unconscious body onto the stretcher and made their way back to the road.

On arrival at the vehicle park they removed the Jeep's keys from Paul's trouser pocket. After bundling him into the back of the Jeep, Banville climbed into the driver's seat and O'Kelly walked to a pickup parked close by. Within two minutes they were on their way to Victoria.

Some five hours later they entered Victoria via Route One from Nanaimo and drove to the building that housed the offices of the Victoria Herald. It was not busy at that time of night and Paul's vehicle was parked facing the front entrance of the newspaper's offices.

One of the assailants then pulled out his cell phone and called Andrew Mortimer, chief editor of the Herald. "Come to the office immediately! There is someone waiting to give you a story. You'll find him in the white Jeep parked at the entrance."

∞

Four

A Visit to the Hospital.
Thursday, 12:45 a.m. 21st September.

Events unfolded quickly after Andrew Mortimer received the call from Paul's assailants. He called Angeline and asked her to meet him at the office, explaining what had transpired.

Angeline was first to arrive and immediately noticed the Jeep parked in front of the building. A minute later Mortimer drove up and stopped alongside her.

The chief editor, a tall, thin man with a trimmed, graying beard, approached the Jeep nervously with Angeline in tow. He could see the still form of a person on the back seat. Gingerly he opened the door and peered at the person's face.

"It's Paul Brinkworth," he said.

"Is he alive?" Angeline asked apprehensively. Andrew felt for a pulse.

"Yes, he has a head wound. We had better get him to the hospital." Angeline felt a lump rise in her throat. "Is that a note attached to his chest?"

Mortimer detached the piece of paper and raised it above his head, trying to catch the soft rays of light from the overhead streetlamp. The message was short but to the point:

This is our last warning. Stop desecrating the rainforest.

"There's no signature to this note," he stated, turning back to the seismologist's inert body. He noticed that an instrument, with a gage, was strapped securely to Paul's right arm and it took a few minutes to remove it.

Angeline gently stroked Paul's hair. "It must be the environmentalists. Paul did say that they threatened him and his friend."

Mortimer opened the driver's side door and removed the keys from the ignition. "This will be a matter for the police to sort out. Let's get him to the hospital."

Together they lifted the unconscious man out of the Jeep and carried him to Mortimer's car.

On their arrival at the emergency room, they placed Paul on a gurney and admitted him. The doctor on duty immediately attended to him, establishing no real damage had been done to his skull. Stitches were required to close the wound and soon the patient was recovering peacefully in a ward.

The doctor had tried to wake him but to no avail. Mortimer attested to the fact that Paul was not a drinker or a drug addict. The doctor speculated some form of drug had been administered to Paul's system to make him sleep and arranged to draw blood for tests.

"He should be okay in the morning. Does he have a family member I can contact?"

Mortimer gave the doctor Paul's home number before they left the hospital. It was already after midnight and the story would have to wait for the morning.

**

Thursday, 6:20 a.m. 21st September.

Paul awoke at 5:30 a.m. the next morning and after a cursory checkup by the doctor he was declared to be fit and healthy. Meg had sat at his bedside the entire night and was ready to take him home. She was red-eyed and stressed out but did not want to ask any questions in front of the doctor. Paul grabbed his clothes from the portable closet next to the bed and quickly got dressed.

Andrew Mortimer had left the Jeep's keys at the hospital reception but Paul felt it wise to not drive himself home so they decided to leave the Jeep in the parking area. "We can pick it up later today when my head's feeling a bit better."

He quickly checked over his vehicle for any damage his assailants might have done but everything seemed in good order so they walked to Meg's SUV and prepared to leave.

Meg cried a few tears as she wound her arms around her husband's neck. They were now out of earshot and she had so many questions. "What happened to you, sweetheart?"

"It's a long story, honey. I'll tell you about it on the way home. Don't worry, I feel fine."

"We were so worried when you didn't come home at the normal time. When Andrew Mortimer called I was beside myself."

Paul explained what had taken place in the rainforest on the previous day as his wife drove them home. Meg listened without interrupting and twenty minutes later they pulled into the driveway.

Paul walked into the kitchen to find Amy had prepared a huge breakfast of bacon, eggs, and toast, and they sat at the table with the children eager to hear his story. After he had eaten, Paul called Margaret at the office to say he would be off for the day—he did not mention his ordeal.

At 9:30 a.m., Andrew Mortimer called to discuss the previous evening's events. Paul, sitting in his leather recliner in the family room, took the call. The dull ache in his head was receding and he was feeling infinitely better.

After the discussion with Andrew, Paul placed a call to the Victoria Central R.C.M.P offices and spoke to the senior inspector in charge, an old golfing friend.

He reported the assault and removal of the seismometer from the monitoring site in Tofino. The inspector promised to follow up with the local environmental groups and was relieved that Paul had suffered no ill effects from the attack.

Paul hung-up and shuffled to the porch where he could rest in the sunlight streaming through the roof of the solarium. Having a troubled sleep he was awakened by a nightmare—the Earth was shaking beneath his feet and buildings were crumbling, toppling toward him. His mind ranged back to the last tremor experience when he was in the rainforest.

The more he thought about his theory the more agitated he became. It was incumbent on the GSC to deal urgently with the possibility of the impending quake and on impulse he picked up his cell phone to make a call.

The director answered immediately.

Paul commenced with his request. "Regarding the last series of tremors, I believe we need to act very soon in warning the public. I really feel we're in for a major event soon. Is there any hope of getting together this evening to discuss the matter?"

"John Fowler has spent the last two days in Vancouver and is due back tomorrow. The other two may be at home—give them a call. We can meet here at my place, say at seven tonight?"

"Thank you, sir," Paul said, hoping the others would now find his theory more feasible.

The director added, "Andrew Mortimer from the Herald called this morning. He said you had an encounter with environmentalists in the rainforest yesterday—how are you feeling?"

Paul answered reassuringly, "My head still hurts a little, but I'm just fine, thanks. I will be taking the matter up with the R.C.M.P later."

The director responded, "Are you going to lay charges?"

Paul answered, "They can approach whatever environmental groups are operating in our area—although the seismometer was removed from its position in the monitoring station, there was no actual damage done. There were also no witnesses so the attack will be difficult to pin on any particular group."

The director agreed. "We will see what comes of it, but I suggest you do not go back there unaccompanied. We can discuss it tonight."

Paul managed to contact both men who were present for the initial discussion. With Fowler away it was an ideal time for him to persuade them regarding his theory.

They all agreed to meet. Meg was not very happy that her husband was going out in his present condition, but Paul was not perturbed. After a bit of cajoling and bribing with chocolate, Meg taxied Paul to his Jeep at the hospital and then he was on his way to the meeting.

On arrival at the director's home, he noted two other cars at the curb and figured the other members of the director's advisory committee had already arrived.

The director's wife opened the door and led Paul down a long hallway to an office where the others were waiting.

Greetings were followed by small talk about Paul's incident before the four men got down to the business at hand. Paul was grateful Fowler was not present and immediately took the floor to explain his theory and fears.

"Gentlemen, here is a scheduled record of the tremors to date since the first one took place on the 29th August at 8:22 a.m." Paul produced a sheet of paper and read off the information he had collated and recorded.

"The time elapsed between each tremor keeps changing—each event being close to fifty percent less than its predecessor. I repeat the fact—we are due for a major quake here very soon. We're talking about a possible megathrust and it's time we informed the public about the possibility."

The atmosphere was electric. The other men sat in silence, not wanting to voice an opinion as the enormity of Paul's words sank in.

The director gave each person a glance and commented, "It seems reasonable to suspect the plates are on the move again. We have not had a series of tremors like this before and these constant time reductions are ominous—I believe we need to take this theory seriously."

The head of the Marine Geological division looked as though he was about to have a heart attack and mopped his brow with a handkerchief. The other member of the advisory panel sat in contemplative silence.

Paul looked at each in turn. "Gentlemen, we have a decision to make."

The director was never one to make decisions alone. He liked to share the load and if there was consensus of opinion he would invariably go along with it. He looked enquiringly at each one in turn and they all nodded their agreement.

It was decided that Paul would make the announcement to the press via his contact at the Victoria Herald. In conclusion the director asked Paul, "When, in your opinion, do you think the quake will occur?"

"I would say we have roughly forty hours—within the next two days."

"I can't believe we are in for a megaquake so soon," said the head of the |Marine Geological division. "It's not quite like waiting for the next bus to arrive, you know."

After a brief benediction the advisory members departed from the director's home. Fortunately, the throbbing that had persisted in Paul's head during the morning hours was gone.

Apart from some sensitivity around the wound, he felt no ill effects. Before heading home he decided to contact Andrew Mortimer of the Victoria Herald and prepare him for an article to be printed for the general public.

The matter was urgent but the language had to be responsible, without sensational overtones. He confirmed the pre-arranged meeting with Angeline Summers for the following day.

**

Thursday, 6:45p.m. 21st September.

The meeting at the director's home lasted forty minutes. On Paul's arrival back at the house, his mother's car was parked in the driveway.

Paul groaned inwardly as he walked up to the front entrance, preparing for a deluge of questions. His mother hugged him and asked, "Well, son, how did this happen?"

Paul pecked her cheek. "I was the victim of a mugging in the rainforest at Tofino. We have a site there with sensitive instruments that measure ground movement. I had a brush with some environmentalists a little while back—they felt we were destroying the eco system in the area by placing our monitoring site there."

Meg, glad to have her husband home, placed her arm around his waist. "Are you going to lay any charges?"

"I gave the police the name of the man with whom I had the first confrontation, a certain Sean O'Kelly. The environmentalist organizations deny anyone of that name works for them," answered Paul.

"Could you have been mistaken about the name?" his mother asked.

"No, Mom. Tom was with me and he also remembers the name. The same fellow also called the Victoria Herald the following day and spoke to Andrew Mortimer about our operation in the forest. Andrew mentioned the same name."

Paul then proceeded to tell them what had been decided at the meeting that evening.

His mother was deeply concerned. "You actually think the Juan de Fuca and the North American plates are unlocking? Did you have any proof they were locked in the first place?"

Paul sighed. "That has been our understanding for some time as there has been no movement on the continental slope."

Lillian Brinkworth looked dubious. "But no one can predict an earthquake."

"No, you are quite right, Mom," said Paul, wishing he had not brought up the subject. He was not going to get into the discussion of prediction with his mother so he simply closed the matter by saying that experience had taught him to trust his intuition and everyone needed to be prepared. He wrote out a list of things that should be kept near at hand and with no further word on the matter gave it to his mother.

Meg made coffee and brought a tray into the sitting room where they spent the next hour talking about the children and things in general.

**

Friday, 8:00 a.m. 22nd September.

After breakfast the following morning, the children went off to their respective schools, leaving Paul and Meg to chat as he got ready for work.

"Are you absolutely sure there are no ill effects from your ordeal? Shouldn't you take another day off, at least?" she asked.

"I am feeling just fine," he shot back a little defensively. "It's very important they get the correct perspective on our work."

Meg backed off. "Fine, love—just take care of yourself."

Paul smiled and said, "Sorry, Honey. I don't mean to sound like a hard-ass but if the Press don't get the right impression of what we're doing it could show us in a bad light. I had better get going."

Paul kissed her, said goodbye, and headed for the Geoscience Centre. He felt a measure of excitement as he contemplated the prospect of entertaining the attractive news reporter from the Victoria Herald.

Paul drove into the center's parking lot, his eye scanning the vehicles to see if she had arrived. Their meeting had been scheduled for eight thirty.

She drove a blue Ford Mustang previously, but there was no Mustang to be seen, so he decided to wait before going into the office. If at all possible, he needed to avoid Fowler.

At exactly 8:30 a.m., Angeline arrived and parked her vehicle next to Paul's Jeep. He felt his pulse quicken as he came around the back of his vehicle, his hand extended in greeting. She continued to hold his hand while she questioned him about the head wound and how he was feeling, releasing her grip only when he turned to lead the way in the direction of the main reception. He was conscious that his cheeks were glowing again, feeling the captivating net of her charm as it slowly spread its net over him.

"Have you seen the morning news, Paul?" She handed him a folded newspaper she carried in her hand.

He realized the pending earthquake had been pushed to the back of his mind.

"Let's have a look at how responsible you've been in making this report," he said lightheartedly, unfolding the newspaper to read the front page headlines.

BE PREPARED! VICTORIA SEISMOLOGIST WARNS OF IMPENDING EARTHQUAKE WITHIN THE NEXT FORTY- EIGHT HOURS.

Paul read on to make sure the news stated the uncertainty of the matter due to the fact it was impossible to scientifically predict an earthquake.

The theory had been correctly reported and the article issued a list of things to do should the event occur. An action plan and what to keep on hand in preparation for the aftermath had also been included.

The need to avoid panic had been stressed and the public was assured of the readiness of the various emergency organizations to cope in the event of a disaster.

He folded the paper and gave it back to her, complimenting her journalistic effort, his only reservation being the unpredictable reaction of the readers.

"The last big quake that hit the island was in 1946. It measured just over seven on the Richter scale, but I have a feeling we are in for a much bigger one this time," Paul said.

"How big?" Angeline asked as they walked along a corridor that led to where the hydrographic surveys were monitored and the oceanographic research took place.

"Well, if the North American and Juan de Fuca plates are parting company, it could result in what we call a megathrust quake."

Paul was enjoying her attention and was tempted to take the opportunity to impress her with his knowledge.

"That could be anything upward of eight on the Richter scale. Scientists are convinced this region has been due for something like this for some time."

Paul sensed her interest in the subject and continued to elaborate.

"The Richter scale shows an exponential growth in magnitude. For instance, if a magnitude of one represented a sphere with a diameter of a golf ball, then the 1906 earthquake of San Francisco would have a sphere with a diameter of three football fields. A megathrust is many times greater than that."

Angeline's attractive face paled slightly as she contemplated the prospect. They looked at the various wall charts and pictures in the area with Paul explaining their relevance.

At times their arms touched as they stood side by side. Neither wanted to move away from the other, both enjoying the moment, not wanting the tour to end. Paul sensed she was as attracted to him as he was to her.

After they had toured the Earthquake Studies subdivision, they wandered down to the docks to see the oceanographic vessels moored there.

"I really envy your way of life—out in the open air when you want to be. I hate having to work in an office when the sun is shining," Angeline stated wistfully.

"It has its down side, believe me. Think of me having to check on the instruments in the forest during winter when it's raining."

Angeline gave a mock shiver. "I guess you're right. I would love to see more but it's getting late."

They walked slowly back to Angeline's parked car. She unlocked the door of the vehicle and turned, placing her hand on his forearm. For what seemed like an eternity, they looked at each other, not saying anything.

"Will I see you again?" Paul murmured, as she slid behind the wheel of the Mustang. He was aware of a dry mouth and his thumping heart reverberating in his eardrums.

She turned the ignition and looked up at him with a smile. "I certainly hope so but I'm not sure if it would be wise."

Paul said nothing. He raised his hand and waved as she backed out, then pulled away. With some alarm, it dawned on him that within twenty-four hours, life on the island could change radically. He walked passed Margaret's office to his own. A report with an accompanying graphic display waited on his desk with one sentence:

Tremor this morning at 02:38 a.m.

∞

Five

An Incomplete Theory?
Saturday, 11:45 p.m. 23rd September.

Paul was squinting at the bedside clock to establish the time, when a realization suddenly dawned. There had, to his knowledge, been no further tremors. Unable to sleep he slipped quietly out of the bed and went downstairs to his study to fire up the laptop and connect remotely to the GSC system. He checked the most recent data available from the Island's seismic monitoring grid but found no evidence of any further tremors since the early Friday morning event—a total of approximately forty-five hours having elapsed without a tremor, which was not in keeping with the normal reduction of time differences previously experienced.

Was the theory incorrect? Perhaps the Juan de Fuca and North American plates had jammed up again, delaying the inevitable.

He would be extremely relieved if the theory turned out to be wrong, despite the certainty of the media's criticism. They would dissect his career and bring discredit to the Center despite all the good intentions. Yet a nagging feeling remained with him —the Big One was still coming.

He sat behind his desk and went through the list of things he'd already taken care of. Canned foods and water were amongst the most important provisions everyone should keep on hand at all times. A first aid kit, a flashlight and blankets rolled up inside sleeping bags were included for each member of the family.

Earthquake preparedness was like breathing air for Paul Brinkworth. Ever since his early schooldays, after seeing a film called Mega Quake, he held seismic upheavals in awe.

He had kept records of all the major quakes around the world, documenting their magnitudes and had known more about the different types of sound waves involved than any of his peers.

In college Paul started a blog about preparedness—always willing to discuss any seismic disturbance with anyone who would talk about it. A regular national annual conference on earthquake prediction had appointed him the chair and had become his favorite gathering of the year.

The Jeep Cherokee had everything required for the aftermath of a disaster. Its four-wheel-drive powered by a strong V8 engine was a match for the worst type of terrain.

Paul's eye caught the unopened evening paper on the corner of the desk. Removing it from the plastic bag, he unfolded it and perused the front page. The bold headline print immediately stood out.

"REACTION TO QUAKE WARNING"

Residents of Vancouver Island received a warning yesterday of a potentially large earthquake in the Juan de Fuca area with mixed emotions. A quake registering high on the Richter scale could have devastating results for the island's cities.

A reporter was commissioned to approach the general public of Victoria in order to test reaction to the report. He summed up after speaking to over fifty people in three different suburbs: "Most of the people appear to have taken a fatalistic approach to the news. No one felt it was necessary to leave the area... "

Paul shrugged as he read the report and was relieved that the news had not caused panic. After all, earthquake possibility is a fact people of the region lived with every day of their lives.

The unpredictability of such an event appeared to detract from the impending reality. The general consensus was to be prepared and cross the bridge when you came to it.

He left the study and climbed the stairs to the bedroom, conscious of a nagging feeling in his gut.

The tremors may have stopped but it did not mean the plates could not suddenly break free without further warning. He slipped into bed and was asleep within minutes.

**

Sunday morning, 24th September.

Early Sunday morning Tom Wilson was suddenly awake. He was not sure if the cat had jumped onto the bed or whether Gertrude had kicked him as she was turning over. A quick glance at the alarm clock confirmed it was still a little early to rise but he decided to get up anyway.

He shuffled through to the bathroom to perform the usual ablutions, his mind focusing on the events of the previous day. It was his personal opinion that a pressure variation in the subduction zone was the most likely cause of the sudden absence of tremors.

"Why are you up so early, darling?" Gertrude sat up in bed and yawned.

"I couldn't sleep any more, Gertie. I think the cat woke me. I've been thinking about the absence of tremors since Friday night and I am of the opinion that a pressure variation is the cause—I still think we could be in for the Big One," Tom answered, preparing to step into the shower.

Gertrude quickly made her opinion known. "Nonsense, love! Paul, as usual, likes to sensationalize everything. His theory just didn't work out. You shouldn't encourage him."

"You don't understand, Gertrude. There is more than a ninety percent chance he's right. It won't do any harm to prepare."

"Oh, fiddlesticks! I think you're both making a mountain out of a molehill."

"Cut it out, Gertie. I'm still going to prepare just in case. I've bought some supplies to replenish our kit but I can't seem to find the flashlight. Do you know where it is?"

"It's on the top shelf above the washing machine."

"Thanks," said Tom, stepping into the shower.

A few minutes later, toweled off and dressed, Tom walked through to the kitchen to start breakfast. He put two eggs on to boil and went to the laundry in search of the flashlight.

It was where Gertrude said it should be. He found an old canvas sports bag that had been used for his tennis accessories and packed canned foods he purchased the previous day.

He then went into the garage and found an empty plastic pop bottle which he filled with water before dumping it into the bag. A small butane stove, used for camping trips was next, followed by two boxes of matches.

Gertrude came to the kitchen and turned on the kettle for the early morning coffee. After removing the boiled eggs she sat at the table and folded her arms, watching her husband check everything he had placed in the sports bag.

"Don't let the kids see what you're doing. I don't want them upset."

"Whatever you say, Gertie. I need to call Paul and discuss the issue."

Gertrude rolled her eyes. "Don't be so negative. There isn't going to be an earthquake."

"You seem very sure of yourself," Tom responded.

"I just don't think Paul can make such an assumption. We'll be fine."

*

Paul was already up and dressed when Tom phoned at eight o'clock.

They discussed the sudden absence of tremors and the possible causes. Both men agreed that a variation of pressure buildup in the subduction zone could be the reason. Both felt the theory of the unlocking plates was still very valid.

Paul commented in conclusion, "I'll deal with the press tomorrow if they contact me to ask about the sudden termination of the tremors. We need to convince the public there is still a very present danger."

Tom agreed and the conversation ended. They would contact each other the next day, if there was no further event within the next twenty-four hours.

Paul and Meg decided to take the children to visit Butchart Gardens, one of Victoria's iconic tourist destinations, for a day out. At 4:10 p.m., the ground shook for fifteen seconds, enough for people in the cafeteria to comment with surprise.

Paul immediately picked up his cell phone and called Tom, who answered immediately.

"That one had a little more magnitude than all the previous tremors. I think we need to prepare for the worst."

Tom concurred. "The subduction zone is definitely on the move. I would love to be able to check on the instruments at Tofino again, if possible."

"If nothing big happens by tomorrow we could do that. I am due to check those instruments anyway. Are you lecturing or can you get away for the day?" Paul responded.

"If nothing has happened by then I'll take time off. I have a class at three but I can ask my colleague to take it," Tom answered with a measure of excitement.

The two men settled the issue and ended their conversation. Meg looked wistfully at Paul knowing he would want to leave the Gardens and return home to connect remotely to the GSC network and check the tremor's magnitude.

**

Monday morning, 25th September.

There had not been another tremor, or major event, since the two men had spoken the previous day. Paul picked Tom up at his home as previously arranged but needing cash, made a quick trip to a bank in a nearby mall.

The two men walked up to the A.T.M outside the bank, hoping to find it deserted, however, several people were lined up waiting. A man wearing a tweed jacket was using the machine while two teenagers, immediately behind were waiting impatiently for him to finish. Paul stood in line while Tom walked to an adjacent shop and peered into the display window.

Paul looked again at the back of the man who was drawing cash from the machine. Something about the tweed jacket caught his attention—he was sure he had seen it before.

The man, who was waiting for his cash, turned to look at the teenagers. He gave them an assuring nod that he would not be long.

For a brief moment Paul saw the man's face. Recognition was instantaneous and he caught his breath. It was Sean O' Kelly, the environmentalist who had confronted them in the rainforest the previous week.

For a brief second he froze, not knowing what to do. Turning toward Tom, he silently gesticulated hoping to attract his friend's attention. When Tom finally noticed Paul trying to signal him, Sean O'Kelly had moved off toward his car in the mall parking area.

"What's wrong?" Tom whispered, as he approached Paul.

"Do you see the man getting into that car? Do you recognize him?"

Tom squinted at O'Kelly preparing to drive away.

"Is that the Irish guy who spoke to us in the forest at Tofino?" Tom asked.

"Yeah, that's him—might also be the jerk who slugged me when I was up there last Wednesday," Paul said, gingerly fingering the wound on the back of his head.

"Shall we call the police? Did you get a look at the vehicle's license plate?" Tom blustered excitedly. "The police could use it to trace the real owner and give us a lead on the swine!"

"Unfortunately, I wasn't able to see the numbers, but it's a gray Honda with sporty rims, a description that probably fits about a thousand vehicles in

Victoria. We should follow him to see where he goes. If we involve the cops at this point, we'll never find out what he's up to. Let's go."

Tom was too flustered to answer as he instinctively obeyed his friend's instructions. They clambered into the Jeep and with a screech of tires, set off in hot pursuit of the Honda, which stopped at the traffic light, down the road.

"What if he's on his way to Tofino?" Tom questioned. "Don't you think it's a matter for the police to take care of?"

"Relax, Tom. We're only going to see where the guy goes. If he's on his way to Tofino, we'll follow him all the way, since we are going there anyway. If he's not a member of an environmental organization then we can find out what outfit he's working for."

Glancing at his watch Tom held onto his seat as Paul swerved around slower moving traffic to stop behind the vehicles at the light.

They had been at a standstill for a few seconds when the lights changed to grccn, allowing the lines of cars to slowly move again.

After overtaking several cars, Paul kept a two-vehicle distance between the Jeep and the Honda. O'Kelly did not appear to be in a hurry. Turning right at the next intersection it became apparent he was heading for the N1, north.

They continued to follow the Honda staying safely behind and so completely focused was their attention on the car ahead that neither spoke a word.

*

It was twelve thirty by the time Paul and Tom entered Port Alberni. O' Kelly kept a steady pace, continuing through the town.

Suddenly Tom broke the silence. "No sign of anymore tremors or a quake! Maybe the theory is wrong after all and we've stirred up a hornet's nest for nothing."

"You may be right, but I still have that gut feeling it's too soon to exclude the theory. The tremors appeared to have stopped but that doesn't mean there's nothing taking place down there," Paul concluded. "It could be ready to blow at any time."

Tom remained silent, hoping that Paul was wrong in his assumption. The excitement surrounding their expectancy of the shaker had spawned a growing anticipation of something pending. If the earthquake struck the island while they were in the Tofino area, there would be a very real danger of a tsunami wiping out everything along the coast of the island.

The winding road ahead began to increase in gradient as the Jeep approached the more mountainous terrain between Port Alberni and Ucluelet. A shallow stream, parallel to the road, flowed peacefully along, a beautiful scene of tranquility.

Paul, attention fully taken up by the twists and turns in the road, made no further comments. The Irishman was pulling away from them and he had to increase the Jeep's speed to maintain the following distance. He glanced at the dash-clock—1:30 p.m.

After they entered the Pacific Rim National Park, six miles before Tofino, O'Kelly turned off into the rainforest parking area. Paul decided not to drive in for fear that O'Kelly might recognize them. He pulled over on the side of the road.

"Why are you stopping?" Tom asked nervously.

"I have a feeling he will park his vehicle and walk back to the highway in order to cross over to the boardwalk. If we drive in there now he'll spot us."

"Do you think he's going to the site?" Tom asked tentatively. "It just occurred to me that Mr. O'Kelly might not be who he says hc is. If he doesn't work for a known environmental group, then there might be another reason why he wouldn't want us puttering around at the monitoring site."

"What do you think he might be up to, then?" Tom asked.

"I'm not sure, but it's something out of the ordinary, and our site is close to it. Our presence represents a threat and we need to check it out," Paul said, leaning forward to peer through the windshield.

As they sat waiting in silence, O'Kelly, having parked his vehicle, appeared at the roadside. After glancing left and right, he crossed the highway to the boardwalk and disappeared into the forest.

Both men, eager to keep the Irishman in sight, jumped out of the Jeep and jogged toward the forest footpath. About fifty yards before the entrance, a car approaching from behind, gave two honks. The vehicle slowed and drew alongside them. A woman spoke through the open window.

"Hey, Paul, what are you guy's doing?"

Paul and Tom stopped dead in their tracks and stared. It was a brief second before Paul recognized the driver. "Angeline! What on Earth are you doing up here?"

"I tried to call you this morning," Angeline answered. "Your secretary thought you might have gone home, so I called there and your wife answered. She said you had gone off with a friend to Tofino."

"Why did you want to speak to me?" Paul persisted, not knowing if he was pleased or concerned at her presence.

"I thought I would take a look at the area, maybe with the hope that you would show me the monitoring site."

Paul stared at her and was at a loss for words until Tom nudged him, indicating he deserved an introduction. "Oh, I'm sorry. This is Tom Wilson, a colleague and friend. Tom lectures at the university on planetary sciences."

Angeline stretched her hand out in greeting. "Hi, Tom—I'm Angeline Summers."

Tom returned the greeting, obviously taken with Angeline's striking looks. He couldn't take his eyes off her for several moments and just stood staring, until she smiled broadly and released his hand.

"I'm going to park my vehicle, so please don't run off without me," she chirped happily and pulled away in the direction of the parking area.

Paul stood motionless as he took stock of the situation.

"What are we going to do now? This could become quite dangerous. She won't back off, no matter what I say."

Tom stuck his hands into his pockets. "Then let her come. It would be great to have her along. These jerks might think twice about tackling three of us."

Paul looked thoughtful. "I don't like it, but I guess there's nothing I can do to stop her."

The two men continued to the rainforest pathway that led to the boardwalk, where they waited for Angeline.

She was wearing tight blue denims and a gray sweater, showing off her curvaceous figure—Tom, bringing up the rear couldn't take his eyes off her. Paul took the lead and headed deeper into the forest, paying keen attention to the path ahead in case he spotted the Irishman.

Angeline drew alongside Paul and smiled at him. "We haven't had any more tremors lately. Do you think the danger for a quake has passed?"

Paul took his time to answer her. "No, I think there is a possibility of a pressure buildup, variation in the subduction area. There is still a strong possibility the plates could break free from one another at any time."

As they walked, her eyes met his, conveying a hint of admiration and promise.

Tom had now overtaken them and was in the lead and with the occasional appreciative backward glance at Angeline, set a quick pace in the direction of the site.

They arrived at the point of departure from the boardwalk and began to wend their way through the thick undergrowth, sometimes sinking a few inches into the forest floor, squelching along the crude path.

It took longer than usual to get to the seismic station. Nothing had been disturbed. Everything still lay scattered over the tiny opening of cleared forest, just as the thieves left it. The police had been there, but had not touched anything, pending further investigation.

Paul looked at his watch. 3:35 p.m. They needed to probe a little deeper into the forest.

He turned to Angeline and said, "We spotted that O'Kelly fellow this morning in Victoria and followed him. He ended up here a few minutes before you arrived—he has to be somewhere in this area."

"We need to look for anything that appears suspicious—a new path or any place that could serve as a habitation or a shelter," Paul whispered. "I don't really know what to expect, but I have a gut feeling they're up to something they shouldn't be."

Tom and Angeline nodded their agreement. They fanned out a little, keeping each other in sight, taking care not to disturb the surroundings. A late afternoon breeze had sprung up, rustling the tree canopy above them.   Angeline made the first discovery.

∞

Six

Back in the Forest.
Monday, 4:00 p.m. 25th September.

Angeline called softly to Paul and pointed to something at her feet. He motioned Tom to follow him and within seconds they were beside her. It was a well-worn path, meandering through the tall trees and dense undergrowth.

They followed it with Paul immediately taking the lead, followed closely by Angeline and Tom. Cautiously, they forged ahead for several minutes until Paul stopped and crouched, motioning for the others to do the same.

Angeline moved behind him and whispered, "What is it? Can you see something?"

Paul turned his head slightly toward her while keeping his eyes fixed on a point twenty yards ahead. The sparse light filtering through the canopy was fading quickly, making it difficult to see much in the gloom.

"There's a wooden structure up ahead, covered with plastic sheeting. Look over there to the side of that big tree. It's difficult to see because of the camouflaged netting draped over it."

"Well, I'll be darned," Tom said, as he peered over Angeline's shoulder. "Someone's doing something illegal here, that's for sure."

As the three squinted into the shadowy undergrowth, the noise of a small generator floated on the air.

At the same time, Sean O'Kelly broke through the foliage next to the camouflaged shelter and strode down the path toward them. He was talking to some unknown person in the shelter and did not see them as they took evasive action, hiding in the dense undergrowth. Sitting side by side, not daring to breathe, they watched until O'Kelly disappeared from view.

Paul beckoned the others to follow and pushed his way through the foliage in a semicircle, toward the shelter. As they drew near, they saw the entrance to another structure that had thick, opaque plastic sheeting drawn tightly over its beams.

"Wait here while I sneak up and take a closer look," Paul whispered, as he felt for the flashlight in the side pocket of his jacket.

"Please, be careful, Paul. Whoever is in there could have a gun." Angeline gripped his arm—he sensed her fear. He responded by stroking her cheek with the back of his fingers, then turned and melted into the thick foliage.

When Paul drew close to the building, he saw a small area of foliage had been cleared to accommodate a further structure. Conflicting thoughts flashed through his mind—it could be some sort of experiment the park's board was conducting, but then why was the presence of the seismic station a threat? The board had granted permission for the instruments to be placed there.

He walked silently along the side of the structure coming across a roughly made door. The wooden frame was covered with the same plastic on the walls. Cautiously he pushed the door open. A strange smell accosted his nostrils.

Stepping inside, Paul saw a makeshift shelving unit against the far wall. On it were cartons stacked one on top of the other, labeled 'Bath Salts'. He crept toward the shelving unit keeping an eye on the door at the same time, hoping no one would enter.

This is some sort of laboratory, he thought as he removed a carton from the middle shelf, opening the unsealed flaps for a peek inside.

Rows of round, plastic bottles with screw-off tops had been neatly packed into the box, each bottle appearing to have its own label. Paul lifted a bottle out for closer inspection and read the label—BATH SALTS, and underneath in smaller print: HURRICANE CHARLEY.

Engrossed in trying to read the fine print on the bottle's label, his focus strayed from his surroundings. In turning his head slightly, he vaguely caught sight of someone standing behind him. Paul turned to face the person—it was a well-built, taller man with an unshaven face. A scar ran from his chin to his left temple, disappearing into shoulder length, untidy black hair. He wore a dirty blue denim shirt with matching jeans.

They stared at each other for half a second before Paul took the initiative and swung his fist at the man's jaw, catching him squarely on the chin. An intense pain shot up Paul's arm as he landed the blow and the man fell against a table and onto the floor.

He didn't wait for any further introductions but jumped over the stunned figure and shot out of the lab. He plunged on through the undergrowth, back to where Tom and Angeline were waiting. "Run! We've been discovered!"

They didn't need any more prompting. Adrenaline coursed through their veins, catapulting them down the path and in the direction of the road.

By the time they reached the end of the boardwalk at the road's edge, all three where tiring and gasping for breath. They stopped for a quick rest, each sucking in the cool, afternoon air with great noisy gulps.

Across the highway, Sean O'Kelly had returned from the vehicle park and was waiting for the traffic to abate before crossing the road. They stood looking at each other in surprise and for interminable seconds no one moved. Suddenly the Irishman reached into his jacket pocket and pulled out an automatic pistol, keeping it concealed with his other hand.

Paul froze, uncertain as to what action he should take. There was a break in the traffic and they stood indecisively, looking at each other.

At that very moment a strange sound started to rise above the sound of the distant traffic and constant rustle of the breeze through the treetops. Paul looked up to see if a jet was passing overhead but there were only scattered clouds—the noise rapidly increased, reaching a deafening crescendo.

Despite having never heard this before he instinctively knew what it was. Many years of training had shaped his understanding and recognition came with a wave of intense fear, paralyzing his muscles.

As the huge primary seismic wave shot through the lithosphere from the subduction area, the earth beneath them began to buck and heave like a wild rollercoaster.

Trees were falling and he felt the ground level rising, throwing him sideways, rolling him first in one direction, then another. Paul caught a brief glimpse of the vehicles in the vehicle park being tossed like toys.

He tried to focus on his two friends. He could not get a good view of either Angeline or Tom as the debris and dust flew in the air about them.

He was concerned for their well-being—in a brief instant he thought of the other people walking in the rainforest and wondered how they would fare.

He thought of children who might be injured or frightened during the shaking of the earth and the falling of trees—he wanted to tell them not to be scared, but there was nothing he could do. Everyone was at the mercy of the seismic monster.

Sean O'Kelly was thrown to the ground. His pistol disappeared into a cavern that opened in the road between them and he slid toward the opening, unable to stop. The Big One had arrived with a vengeance.

**

Monday afternoon, minutes after the quake.

The noise was deafening and the shaking seemed to go on forever. In vain, Paul tried to get onto his feet. He was conscious throughout the entire two and half minutes of seismic violence. It had seemed like an eternity.

Finally, when the shaking stopped, Paul lay where he had fallen. The thudding sound of trees crashing to the ground continued after the Earth's rumbling ceased. Then silence—no sounds of bird life or rustling leaves in the late afternoon breeze.

He slowly lifted his head and a sight of total destruction greeted him. The once proud forest with its lush undergrowth had become a tangled mass of green and brown. Nothing moved in the ensuing aftermath.

Paul looked around him in utter dismay. Conscious of the breeze on his face, he shuddered, trying to will the feeling back into his numbed body. Rolling onto his stomach, he got onto his hands and knees to see what fate had befallen the others.

Tom was lying under the branch of a tree that had fallen across the path. He was stirring and appeared to be unhurt.

Angeline had been thrown to the side of the road, ending up in the ditch. A shallow fissure had opened in the middle of the road, running southward across the devastated highway, disappearing into the forest on the ocean side.

Paul saw no sign of O'Kelly. Nor had anyone appeared out of the undergrowth of the forest in pursuit of them.

Angeline began to stir, raising herself on one elbow. As her eyes strained to focus she saw Paul, apparently unharmed, standing unsteadily to his feet. Without uttering a word they stared at each other, both in a state of shock.

Paul stood slowly, shaking off bits of gravel and broken twigs from his clothing. He limped to Angeline, hampered a little by the old leg injury.

She attempted to stand but her legs were too weak to support her. Paul instinctively put his arms protectively around her, drawing her close to him. She began to shake and sob gently.

"It's okay, Angie—you're safe now."

She managed a short sentence. "What happened?"

Even as she asked the question her mind started to comprehend the facts.

Tom managed to extricate himself from his arbor prison and stood in awed silence, surveying the carnage.

"Are you hurt, Angie?" Paul asked tenderly, as he brushed the hair away from her eyes.

She shook her head. "No, I'm all right. I guess we've just experienced the Big One?!"

Paul glanced at his friend. "You okay, Tom?"

"Yeah, I'm fine. A little bruised and shaken but no broken bones. We had better make tracks and get out of here. We're pretty close to the sea and I suspect in a short time we could be facing a tsunami."

Paul took Angeline's hand and they began jogging down what was left of the road.

"We need to get to the Jeep as quickly as possible. If it's still in one piece, there's a good chance we can get out of here," Paul commented with a measure of confidence in his voice.

"What about my car?" Angeline asked breathlessly.

"Leave it for the time being, Angie. We have very little time—a four-wheel drive is our best bet," Tom commented.

Paul scanned the devastation ahead, hoping to see the vehicle. Angeline, having recovered her composure, struggled to keep up with him, her hand tightly clutching his like a small child.

"How far are we from the ocean?" she asked.

Light was beginning to fade quickly and Paul groped for the flashlight in his pocket while Tom answered her question.

"About five hundred, maybe seven hundred yards."

The three survivors climbed over dozens of split tree trunks, broken branches, and jagged paving until they reached the area where they had left the Jeep.

"I can't see the vehicle anywhere," Tom groaned.

"Keep looking. I'm sure it can't be more than twenty or thirty yards ahead. It's probably covered with fallen trees and broken branches."

"There it is!" Angeline pointed. "Over there, on the left."

Though the Jeep was not where it had originally been parked, miraculously, it was still on its wheels.

There was a fallen tree lying close to the vehicle, with its branches covering a part of the roof, however, there appeared to be only light damaged to some of the paintwork.

Despite its white color, the Jeep had been difficult to see in the fading light. They freed it of the fallen debris, inspecting front, back, and underside for any further damage.

"Let's get going," shouted Paul, turning the key in the ignition. "We don't have much time to get to higher ground. It will be impossible to see the wave when it strikes."

"Can you be sure a tsunami will hit the island?" Angeline asked pensively.

Paul glanced at her. "Yeah, I'm sure."

"How long will it take to reach us?" she queried nervously, slumping into the backseat.

In the passenger seat, Tom turned to her. "Tsunami's are always generated by earthquakes that take place due to subduction. We haven't experienced an ordinary quake here, though."

Paul added, "This was definitely a megathrust—it probably released most of its energy along the fault line out to sea."

"Tsunamis travel at about 450 mph and are only about three feet high in the open water. When the height of water, between the sea bed and the surface gets less as it approaches land, the wave gets taller," Tom concluded.

"But how long do we have?" Angeline's voice had become almost a whisper.

Both men were quiet as the Jeep lurched and rolled over the destroyed roadway—each were furiously trying to calculate an answer.

The plate movement would influence the ocean immediately above it. Also to consider would be the possible blowout of energy along the megathrust fault zone into the Pacific Ocean.

Paul said, "We could have as little as ten minutes and as much as twenty. Let's hope the road farther up is in a better condition than this—these fallen trees are almost impossible to get through."

Tom was convinced the Alberni Highway would be better, as there was less forest and more hills. Plus they headed away from the sandy coastal area and onto the main bedrock of the island.

The fallen trees became fewer, making their progress easier. The Jeep, with its powerful 5.2 liter motor and continuous four-wheel drive, was making short work of the difficult terrain. Paul was a picture of concentration as they negotiated deep cracks and fissures ripped open by the quake's force.

He had to be particularly careful of areas where liquefaction had taken place, but to that point in time, the race against the potential tsunami appeared to be going well.

Paul checked the dash clock. With the tsunami in mind he made furtive glances in the direction of the sea. The Jeep crawled through large breaks in the paving, sometimes as deep as three feet.

Finally they reached the Port Alberni turn-off and Paul gratefully turned toward higher ground. Thirteen minutes had elapsed since leaving the rainforest parking area.

"We're almost out of danger from the water," said Paul, managing a weary grin.

He knew they would have to be at least two miles inland to escape the fury of the wave. With the improving road surface, he thrust the accelerator to the floorboard. The Jeep reared up like a stallion in response, the fuel injection system ramming fuel into the eight cylinders, delivering an explosive power to the wheel train.

Angeline kept casting frightened glances out of the back window, expecting, at any moment, to see a monstrous deluge of water racing toward their retreating vehicle.

"There's something strange happening back there," Angeline sputtered, trying to focus her eyes on the farthest distance the gathering gloom would allow.

"What is it, Angie? What can you see?" asked Paul.

Tom turned in his seat and squinted into the semi-light behind them.

Angeline kept staring until it happened again—"I think someone's following us! There may be a vehicle a few miles behind us. I see a glow of lights every now and then—possibly a car's headlights."

Paul and Tom looked at each other but said nothing.

**

Monday, 4:40 p.m. 25th September.

O'Kelly shook his head to clear his vision. The fury of the earthquake had abated, leaving him in a state of shock and disbelief.

At first he thought someone had thrown a bomb at them but when he looked upward and saw the rim of the four-foot deep crater, he realized the cause could not have been explosives. He would definitely not have survived a blast that could rip a hole into the earth the size of the one he was in.

He got slowly to his feet. It was only when he peered over the rim of the fissure that he realized what had actually happened.

The devastation around him was almost unbelievable—he had just experienced his first earthquake. A feeling of strange wonderment came over him—was it a dream?

Thankful for his survival, he considered how fortunate he had been. Then a noise from the forest came to his ears. The sound of grunting and cursing broke the eerie silence.

O'Kelly stared in the direction of the boardwalk and to his surprise a man burst out of the devastated forest and lurched onto the roadway. It was Andre Banville. Banville was still rubbing his swelling jaw as he approached O'Kelly.

"You okay, Sean?" the man called out as he spotted O'Kelly's head sticking above the rim of the crevice.

"Yeah, a little shaken but in one piece," answered O'Kelly. "You?"

Banville gingerly rubbed his jaw. "That motherfucker, Brinkworth; the one I slugged on the head—was snooping around the lab. I crept up on him but he turned around and threw a punch which caught me off-balance."

"Do you think he knows what we are doing?" asked O'Kelly.

"He had a bottle of Hurricane Charley in his hand. I guess that would raise his suspicion."

O'Kelly gave Andre an angry look and said, "Rushmore is going to be fucking pissed about this. Help me look for the gun. We don't have much time."

After finding the weapon, they scrambled toward the parking area.

There were only a few cars and these had been strewn around like toys in a sandpit, with only one or two still on their wheels. O'Kelly looked for his own car and found it upside down and under two other vehicles. Within a couple minutes he found an old four-wheel drive Land Cruiser still intact and on its wheels.

"Here's one we can use. Do you know anything about hot-wiring?"

"Yeah, we should be able to force the window down—I see the owner left it slightly open."

Banville placed his hands against the driver side window and pushed downward. It opened enough for him to get his arm through, allowing him to grab the door handle. He opened the door and pulled out the ignition wires from beneath the steering wheel. Within two minutes the engine started.

There had been no other sign of life and they assumed the owners of all the vehicles were still somewhere in the forest.

"We've got to get out of here as quickly as possible," O'Kelly shouted. "A tsunami could be on its way toward us."

"How do you know?" Banville asked fearfully, holding on for dear life as the vehicle bucked and heaved over the myriad of obstacles, strewn in its path.

O'Kelly glanced briefly at his comrade. "Holy shit dude—what have you been smoking? Everyone knows earthquakes and tsunamis go together."

The Land Cruiser was faring well despite the altered terrain and within fifteen minutes they had reached the turn off to Port Alberni.

"What are we going to do now, Sean?"

"We'll have to deal with Brinkworth and his friends. I have worked too long and hard to lose all I've put into this operation!"

"What do you intend to do with them."

"We have to catch them first. Use your imagination, Andre."

"You mean...kill them!" Andre began to perspire. He had never killed anyone before.

"If we don't kill them, we run the risk of losing the whole operation."

"Shit! I dunno, Sean—murder's a serious business."

"It's them or us. Think about it. The earthquake has actually come at a very convenient time. We'll make it look as though they were victims of falling rock."

"Are you sure they escaped?"

"Of course I'm sure," O'Kelly answered, annoyed.

"Did you actually see them?"

"They were standing right in front of me, across the road when the quake hit us. They couldn't have disappeared into thin air. They must have parked their vehicle up the road. I'm sure they're ahead of us somewhere."

After ten minutes, he picked up the taillights of the Jeep, about a mile ahead. O'Kelly muttered a profanity and increased speed, keeping an eye on shadows and dark patches that appeared in the road.

∞

Seven

Victoria's Disaster Response.
Monday afternoon—the aftermath. 25th September.

Bud Hamlin had been ecstatic when he received the appointment to the position of Emergency Preparedness Officer. It was a first for Vancouver Island. His job was to coordinate the emergency programs for the various communities in the event of a major disaster.

A veteran with fifteen years of service in the Victoria Fire Department, he was an experienced manager of rescue and recovery operations, having personally participated in thirty-three major fires in the Victoria district.

He had taken up his new post with great enthusiasm, drawing on the expertise of veterans in other relevant organizations, such as the Canadian Red Cross, the Emergency Social Services and the Department of National Defense. The beginning of a new Provincial Earthquake Support Plan was in the making. He had no doubt, that in time, they would be able to handle the worst scenario.

Time, however, was not on their side. A plan that was not fully evolved, or ready for action, was no good at all. However, the existing plan was all that stood between the success of a reasonable recovery from any disaster, or its failure.

Bud was in the process of leaving the office in Blanchard Street, a temporary site for Emergency Preparedness Canada, when the Big One arrived.

He had just pulled out of his parking spot and entered the busy viaduct headed for Route 17, the shortest distance home. The weather had become cooler with the approach of the fall season and he looked forward to relaxing before the log fire in the living room.

Bud had been fortunate to find a reasonable break in the traffic, seconds before the quake struck, and was one of the few escapees of the auto-carnage that ensued. Although his Chevy Blazer had been thrown around, it had not flipped, or made contact with any other objects.

When the shaking stopped he sat motionless, stunned and at first, uncomprehending. The reality of disaster slowly sank in as his mind quickly adjusted to disaster response. Plans were theoretical—until an actual event and it took teams of dedicated people to enjoy any measure of success.

The responsibility for that success came crashing down onto his shoulders, galvanizing his thoughts, propelling him into action. In the rear of the vehicle were his emergency battery operated radio transmitter and all the essentials for disaster survival management.

Grabbing a walkie-talkie, he called Raymond Boyd, head of the newly formed Victoria and Districts Disaster Assistance Response Team, or DART, as it was generally called. As he waited for Raymond to reply, he scanned the surroundings, visibly shaken by what he saw. The sight would be imprinted on his mind forever.

"Boyd, here!"

"Ray! I can't believe it's finally happened...what a disaster! We must have been clobbered with a magnitude nine! Most of the buildings here in Blanchard have collapsed and there's chaos everywhere. Are you okay? Can you mobilize?"

"Yeah, I'm in the process of making sure the teams are on their way to the designated meeting places," Boyd responded. "It's going to be heavy going with the condition of the streets and chaotic traffic situation. I'll call you back in a few minutes when everyone's arrived at their destinations to advise you what our numbers are."

"Okay, Ray—you take care now."

Bud proceeded to make contact with various key people, the next being the emergency contact at the Victoria General, the biggest hospital in the city.

"Irene! This is Bud Hamlin from E.P.C. We have a CODE ORANGE on our hands. Can you give me an idea of the hospital's present capability to handle the emergency?"

Irene Bartell, the official in charge of Disaster Response, was still in a state of shock but she managed to stammer out the bad news.

"We are trying to verify the damage to the emergency power supply. There is zero power at the moment and light is being supplied by the back-up battery illumination system. Things are critical in the operating theatres because the back-up system for the equipment has not kicked in. We also have no water. There has obviously been a disruption to the main supply."

"Apart from the problems you've mentioned, has the emergency plan for extra space, care, and provisions been mobilized?"

"Yes, that's all underway as we speak. Our Fire Response Team is helping out on the premises, but they'll be diverted into the field as soon as possible. We'll need extra help with clearing damaged wards and re-situating patients but I'm sure we'll manage."

Bud tightened his grip on the transmitting button.

"At least now we can see if the inter-hospital communication system works adequately. I guess you haven't had much time to practice."

"Not really," Irene responded with an air of uncertainty. "I guess we're in the deep end today."

"Let me know if there's anything I can help with."

"Sure, Bud - thanks for the call."

It was time to see if he could be of assistance to the injured. He needed to stay close to his vehicle so he could listen to the various reports. He also wanted to attempt a drive down to the waterfront to assess the situation there.

It was then he noticed the slight incline of the buildings toward the south end of the island. At first he thought it was his eyesight, but after blinking and rubbing his eyes, he realized the angle of the ground had changed.

He called Raymond Boyd again.

"Hello, Ray? I don't know if you've noticed—but does everything appear to be listing slightly to the south?"

Ray hesitated for a few seconds.

"You're absolutely right. The island has definitely tilted toward the south."

"Do you realize what sort of a problem that will create?"

Ray contemplated the question. "You mean drainage of water and sewerage?"

"Not only that, but road levels, sporting facilities, stairwells, safety of high rises—I could go on!"

"I wonder if we'll ever see a return to normality. It's enough to boggle the brain," said Boyd.

Bud answered, "We have enough to concern ourselves with—I guess it's going to be with us for a long time."

**

Monday, 4:43 p.m. 25th September.

Dan Duplessis was having the time of his life. His old Ford pick-up threatened to dissolve into a mobile scrap yard as it bucked, and lurched at rattle-producing speed, over what remained of Central Saanich Road.

Moments before the earthquake, he had arrived home from work and was looking forward to a relaxing evening in front of the television.

Dan, a native South African, was single, six foot tall and athletically built. He worked as the assistant manager for a vehicle workshop in Central Saanich and ran marathons in his spare time.

Due to Dan's superb physical condition, the recent appointment as a leader to one of Victoria's Disaster Assistance Response Teams had not come as a surprise to his friends. Ray Boyd, who played football with Dan, had approached him to join the team. He had recognized the young South African's dedication, efficiency, and physical fitness.

Now, at the age of twenty-five, Dan owned a house and a magnificent German shepherd named

Sultan, the latter being an inseparable part of his life. Excluding working hours, Sultan was always at his master's side, ready to obey every command.

After the shaking had passed and Dan was able to stand again he saw that the mobile home had shifted off its foundations along with all the others in the park.

Mobiles stood at precarious angles, parked vehicles were strewn all over the place and people were trying to pick themselves up off the ground. Sultan had disappeared during the thirty seconds of seismic violence and Dan eventually found the dog crouching in the back of his pickup, this being the only safe place according to canine psychology.

The pickup had suffered some buffeting, but apart from superficial dents, remained undamaged. The equipment Dan received during his training with DART was in the locked steel box on the back of the truck. Instinctively he knew what he had to do.

He had called Sultan into the cab and set off for the predetermined meeting place.

Each community had six DART members delegated to the task of assisting the injured in a post-disaster situation. Dan was the appointed leader for Central Saanich, one of ten communities covered in the event of any catastrophic occurrence. Saanich Peninsula hospital was the pre-arranged meeting place where the other team members would meet for a quick briefing before dispersing into the various suburbs.

Ray Boyd, head of D.A.R.T and team leader for Victoria, would be in touch with the team leaders by means of his battery operated radio transmitter. The other members had smaller handsets with limited transmitting and receiving radius that would cover the communities they served.

Dan flicked the switch of his transmitter and the familiar crackling sound assured him the set was operating. The correct frequency for contact with Ray had already been pre-set so there would be nothing he could do but wait for Ray to make first contact.

Central Saanich Road had become a mass of broken paving, making travel difficult. There were several cars that had been on the road when the quake took place, the drivers having lost control during the height of the shaking.

Some had plowed into adjacent yards; others into the ditch and one had knocked down a lamppost. The vehicle owners, apart from a state of shock, appeared to be unhurt so he did not stop to assist. His first priority was to make contact with the rest of his team.

The hospital in Mount Newton Cross Road was not far from where he lived. It took eighteen minutes for him to reach the parking area. Sultan barked furiously at everything, his head protruding from the passenger window, saliva flying everywhere.

There was no sign of the other team members but then they had to travel much further to the rendezvous than he did. He climbed out of the truck and surveyed the hospital building, taking note of the extensive damage to one of the wings. There were people scurrying around in a panic, trying to put out a fire in one of the storage rooms.

Others were walking around aimlessly in shock looking for explanations, while doctors and nurses screamed instructions at anyone who would listen.

He quickly checked through his equipment satisfying himself everything was there. At that moment the R/T crackled to life and the deep voice of Ray Boyd boomed into the cab, causing Sultan to tilt his head to one side and growl.

"Boyd calling Duplessis—come in, Danny."

"Reading you loud and clear, Ray."

"What's your twenty?"

"I'm at the pre-arranged meeting place and will be moving into the field as soon as the others come. Our area appears to have been quite severely shaken up and I'm anticipating many casualties, over."

"Yeah, it looks like the island has shifted slightly. Bud Hamlin thinks the magnitude was above nine. I'm at the Victoria rendezvous point—only three in my team have arrived so far. We're going to wait five minutes and then move into the field. Please remember to report every half hour, if possible. Do you copy?"

"Copy that, Ray. Good luck—Danny out."

Ten minutes later Dan's entire team, with the exception of one, reported for duty.

He tried to raise the missing member but to no avail.

"We need to get moving—there's a lot to do. Remember to keep in touch with me and to report every thirty minutes."

The men knew the drill and the designated areas they had to cover. Each had passed a first aid course and had been trained in rescue work, specializing in retrieving the injured from confined areas.

Dan and his designated team member, Brent, hurried to get to the outer extremity of their area before the light failed. Their area covered at least two thousand homes and a few sporadic small businesses. Their progress depended entirely on what they found.

Many places would be empty, as people knew field stations would be set up by the Red Cross organization in various pre-designated areas. General instruction to the community emphasized the need to register at one of these stations, where help would be available.

Using Dan's pickup, the two men drove to Meadowland Drive, the beginning of their area and started knocking on the door of each home, checking on the residents. Most homes had suffered some damage but injuries were generally not serious, shock being the most prevalent. They rounded the comer of a road running parallel to Route 17 and discovered their first major problem.

Dan rolled his window down. "That house is on fire. Look at all the smoke—we had better check up on the occupants."

"The smoke appears much blacker than what would normally result from a house fire," Brent remarked.

"Maybe it's not the house but something in the backyard."

They drove into the driveway and stopped.

Dan knocked on the front door of the home but there was no response. He ran back to the pickup and took a crowbar out of the emergency kit. It took one minute to open the door. A quick search of every room revealed nothing. The occupants were not home. He raced outside, almost colliding with Brent, who was returning from the backyard.

"The yard backs onto the freeway. A rig has crashed through the barrier and the back wheels are on fire."

The two men sprinted around the house. Dan could hardly believe his eyes.

"The rig has something caught beneath it." Brent gazed in horror.

"It's a car. Oh my god," responded Dan as he moved in for a closer look.

His heart sank as he heard a faint cry within the wreckage. The late afternoon sun was dipping below the horizon and it was getting difficult to see into shaded areas. He shone his flashlight in the direction of the cry but could see only twisted metal. Then he directed the light beam onto the rig's cab and saw a man slumped over the steering wheel.

"The driver of the rig appears to have been killed on impact," said Dan.   He then directed the flashlight beam to the wreckage of the second vehicle underneath.

There has to be someone here—unless my ears are deceiving me, he thought, despite the extent of the carnage visible in the light beam.

Not equipped for major firefighting, they knew speed would be essential in any attempted rescue.

Dan climbed up to the cab and yanked on the door.

"We'll have to drag the driver's body clear—give me a hand."

Brent could feel the heat as he joined Dan who was struggling with the seatbelt. The hydraulic brake lines serving the back wheels of the rig suddenly exploded, spraying burning fluid in all directions.

"We don't have much time. It will only take those flames a few minutes to reach the fuel tank!"

They managed to release the seatbelt and drag the body of the driver away from the scene, leaving it on the grass near the backdoor of the house.

Dan snatched up the fire extinguisher, throwing it to Brent and they quickly returned to the wreck.

"Try to retard the fire!" shouted Dan, pointing at the rapidly spreading flames, creeping menacingly toward the fuel tank.

He gave a sharp whistle, bringing a quivering Sultan to his side—Sultan, trained in confined-space rescues, would be helpful in finding where the occupant of the second vehicle was trapped.

Brent continued to subdue the leading flames of the fire but the breeze was fanning the heat into his face. The blaze inched closer with every passing second.

Dan gave Sultan the order to search and the dog immediately dove into the carnage beneath the rig.

"Hang on! Concentrate the spray in one place— don't waste any foam—Sultan appears to have found someone!" Dan yelled.

Sultan barked furiously as he snuffled at the base of the wreckage. He began to paw frantically at an opening in the twisted steel.

Dan crouched to the narrow opening and felt inside. To his astonishment a hand grasped his sleeve and a trembling voice whispered, "Help me, I can't move. I don't want to die!" A feeling of immense relief flooded him.

**

Monday, 5:03 p.m. 25th September.

At exactly 5:03 p.m., the tsunami struck the island, venting its fury on the two hundred and fifty miles of western coastline. The Alaska Tsunami Warning Center in Palmer, Alaska, issued a warning over television and radio but few people, if any on the island, heard it. Traveling at 435 mph the wave approached the island, swiftly growing to thirty yards in height as it reached shallow water closer to the shore.

Overrunning the smaller islands at the entrance to the inlet, it rushed up the waterway to Port Alberni. The towns of Tofino, Ucluelet and Port Renfrew, were engulfed in a matter of seconds.

The towering deluge smashed residences, buildings, and vehicles, totally devastating everything in its path. Limp bodies of people, dogs, cats, rodents were caught up together in the backwash and pulled out to sea, after the wave had surged inland for almost two miles.

The strength of the surge up the main inlet had dissipated by the time it reached Port Alberni, but the water rose enough to cause immense destruction to everything on the banks of the Somas river.

The water flooded onward into the town catching many unprepared. Residence may have known of the possibility that a tsunami would come, but were too busy trying to extricate loved ones and valuables from the partial ruins of their homes. Others were giving thanks they had escaped the clutches of the megathrust and were busy preparing for after-shocks when the wave struck.

Few people living along the shoreline of the coast saw the huge wave coming, the only indication being a loud noise like a clap of thunder, when it crashed on the rocks that fringed the shoreline.

Had O' Kelly and Banville looked behind them after turning onto the Port Albemi road, they might have witnessed the terrifying scene of the water rushing toward them.

It was getting dark and the thought of looking behind did not occur to either of the men. They were totally absorbed with the taillights of the Jeep ahead of them. Fortunately, the water's forward thrust dissipated by the time it overtook the turn-off junction.

The wave reached to within one hundred yards of the Land Cruiser, before retracting to the ocean with a rushing, gurgling sound. The two men would never know that only precious seconds of time had separated them from instant death. Thousands of others had not been that fortunate.

∞

Eight

A Difficult Rescue.
Monday, 5:43 p.m. 25th September.

Dan Duplessis dragged the young girl clear of the wreckage. A check of her vital signs showed, that apart from bad bruising and scrapes, there were no life threatening injuries. He quickly carried her to the back verandah of the house and wrapped her in a blanket.

The flames were licking at the combustible fuel-air zone surrounding the gas tank and only seconds separated the leaking fumes from ignition.

The young girl was too young to be the driver, Dan thought as he returned to the scene to see Sultan crawling into the space he had made earlier with the crowbar. Instinctively he knew the dog had discovered the other person.

It's now or never he thought fleetingly, and lunged toward the opening, avoiding the protrusions of twisted steel that threatened to tear his sweat-covered flesh.

"I can't hold on any longer! The extinguisher's empty!" Brent shouted as he threw the cylinder to the ground and beat a hasty retreat from the developing inferno.

111

Dan didn't waste his breath in answering as he elbow-crawled his way into the small opening under the wreckage. His head came into contact with Sultan's tail-wagging posterior. The shepherd reversed out with someone's jacket in his jaws. Then to Dan's delight he saw the jacket was still attached to its owner, the driver of the SUV.

It was a woman about thirty-five years of age. His heart sank as he saw the ashen color of death written on her face. Sultan was tugging furiously at the body but it appeared the driver's one foot was trapped. The dog was pulling with all his strength, grunting with every tug. Suddenly the trapped foot came free and Dan reached in to grab the jacket, pulling both woman and dog out together.

"Good boy, good boy," Dan shouted.

The dog, however, was unwilling to release the jacket. "Release, Sultan, release! Good dog."

The gas tank exploded with a resounding bang, igniting the diesel fuel and flinging pieces of metal in all directions. The resulting shockwave drove Dan to the ground causing him to let go of the woman but he quickly jumped up onto his feet again. Shielding his face from the heat with one arm, he quickly pulled her to safety.

Brent came to his assistance and they carried the woman to the back verandah. Dan quickly checked her pulse and determined she was still alive.

Without further hesitation they carried her to the pickup. The young girl had started to regain consciousness by the time Dan returned and he helped her to sit up, offering a drink from his water bottle.

"My mother, where's my mother?" She searched his face for some clue.

"She's alive but we must get her to a doctor," Dan answered.

The young girl looked distraught. "What happened to us?"

Dan explained the earthquake must have caused the driver of the rig to lose control and plow into the SUV.

"I don't remember a thing," the young girl responded.

Dan could see shock was setting in. "Relax—I'm going to carry you to my truck."

Brent was sitting in the back, cradling the woman's head in his hands so Dan placed the girl in the passenger seat. He started the engine and took off as fast as the road condition would allow.

Sultan stood barking in the back of the pick-up, blissfully unaware of the emergency.

"What's your name?" he asked her gently.

"Amy—Amy Brinkworth," she replied shakily.

"Where's your father?"

"Mom said he went up to Tofino—he's a seismologist and works at the Geoscience Centre."

113

"Is there some way you can get hold of him?"

"He does have a cell phone but I don't know the number."

The irony of the Brinkworth situation came to Dan's mind. Amy's father doesn't know that his wife has become the victim of the very phenomenon he studied on a daily basis.

*

Dan pulled into the Saanich Peninsula Hospital and parked the pickup near the front entrance. Brent, with Megan Brinkworth's head on his lap, had cushioned her from the bumps as best he could. When the pickup came to a stop he vaulted off the back and ran into the entrance hall to look for a gurney.

He returned to help Dan transport the injured woman into the outpatient's area. People were streaming in and out of emergency reception, making it difficult for the two men to get to the admissions counter.

Dozens of people, milling around the counter, were trying to get information from the two receptionists who were trying to be as patient as possible. Finally they managed to attract the attention of a Registered Nurse, who hurried over and began to monitor Megan's vital signs.

"Do you know what happened to this lady?"

"Vehicle accident on Route 17—rescued her from a situation you wouldn't believe," Dan said.

"Do you know how long ago it happened? Was she unconscious when you found her?"

"We found the wreck about forty minutes ago but I can't say exactly when it happened. My guess is it happened during the earthquake and that was at about four-thirty five."

Dan looked at his watch. "That makes it about an hour and three-quarters, give or take, since their accident."

"If she's been out that long she could have very severe concussion. It may be something much more serious. Who is this?" she asked, pointing to Amy.

"This is Amy. The lady is her mother," replied Brent putting his arm around the young girl. "Is there anyone who can check her over?"

The RN produced a notepad from her pocket. "Sure, I'll take care of her. I expect we're going to be pretty busy tonight. Please fill in a report at the front reception and don't forget to enter their names, the time that you found them and the time you arrived here."

The two men nodded and with thumbs-up to Amy, moved back toward the reception area.

Dan smiled at Amy. "Don't worry, love—the nurse will look after you."

It was going to be a long night for all of them.

**

Monday, 6:10 p.m. 25th September.

Tom was the first to spot the major obstacle in the road.

"There's something ahead of us across the road. I can't quite make it out but it looks like fallen rock."

Paul immediately slowed and brought the Jeep to a stop about ten yards from the obstacle. Tons of fallen rock, the results of a landslide higher up the mountain slope, lay on the road in front of them. They had entered the foothills of the Mackenzie Mountain Range, through which the pass had been skillfully engineered many years before.

A fear of rock-slides had plagued Paul's mind. The road along Kennedy Lake had patches of crumbled paving which had forced him, at times, to drive with extreme caution.

The section from the turn-off up to the lake had been much better, but as the ground began to rise, the going had become more difficult. With the mountains towering above them, the potential for rock-slides had increased dramatically.

"Who could be following us?" asked Angeline.

"It could be O'Kelly," answered Tom.

"It could be anyone, maybe even tourists—I'm sure we were not the only ones in the forest at the time of the earthquake. Besides, I saw O'Kelly slipping into a crevice the quake opened up in the road. I doubt he survived that," Paul interjected.

For obvious reasons, neither of the three wanted to take the chance of waiting for the other vehicle, but in front of them lay a reason for that very possibility.

"Do you think we could get over this?" questioned Tom as the two of them walked to the fallen rocks and surveyed what they could see in the Jeep's headlight beams.

Paul turned his flashlight on the areas of shadow that had been created by outcrops of broken rock, and then climbed onto the rocks to observe the width of the slide.

It appeared that a great deal of the mountain to the right of them had collapsed but only a small portion of it had fallen onto the road. They would have about thirty yards of difficult terrain to cover after climbing the part of the embankment that presented the easiest access to the Jeep.

Having made sure an exit would be possible on the other side, Paul asked Tom to stay on top of the access area with the flashlight to keep a check on the front wheels.

Angeline was to stay behind the vehicle on the roadway and keep an eye on the traction of the back wheels. He had to negotiate approximately five yards of loosely compacted soil that offered purchase to the Jeep's tires. With the driver's window open, Paul gunned the motor and inched the front wheels forward onto the incline.

As he shifted the lever into low-range, Paul realized limited power would prevent the vehicle from sinking into the soil and burying the wheels. He had never done any serious climbing before or put the Jeep to any test on difficult terrain.

The Cherokee bounced a little as the back wheels came off the paving, causing a sideways creep. Paul did his best to compensate. Halfway up the incline the Jeep began to sink into the softer ground and he eased up on the accelerator.

The Jeep then came to a dead stop and he realized he'd made a mistake. Both Angeline and Tom screamed above the noise of the motor, encouraging him to keep the forward momentum going. He immediately overcompensated by ramming the gas pedal to the floor. The wheels bit deeply into the soft soil and began to sink lower, taking all of their hopes with it.

Angeline glanced furtively behind her and could see the glow of the on-coming headlight beams through the trees. The vehicle following was still at a slightly lower elevation but she knew it would not take long for whoever it was to reach the rockslide.

She turned back to watch the Jeep's progress. The rear wheels seemed to be getting hopelessly bogged down but suddenly the tires caught underlying rocks and the vehicle shot forward. The front wheels clawed at the top of the embankment and the Jeep began to inch its way up to the top, the Quadra-Trac system transferring most of the power to the front wheels.

With a whoop, Tom gave Paul a thumbs-up and ran to give Angeline a hand up over the embankment. When the Jeep reached a more horizontal plane, Paul brought it to a standstill. Tom and Angeline gratefully jumped onboard and slid onto the smooth leather seats.

"Well done, Paul—for a moment I thought we were going to be stranded here," said Angeline, full of admiration.

"I was praying," Paul said with a chuckle.

He was grinning from ear to ear as they traversed the thirty yards to the other side of the slide without further incident.

Angeline turned to look out of the back window and said, "The glow from those headlight beams are getting really close now. While you two were busy overcoming the obstacle I've been watching—I believe it's another large vehicle and they are probably arriving on the other side of the rock slide as we speak."

Monday, 7:20 p.m. 25th September.

The front wheels of the Jeep came to a jarring stop on the edge of a drop twenty feet into a ravine. They had been traveling carefully through the mountain pass, maneuvering around the many fallen rocks and occasional tree littering the once proud achievement of the island's road engineers.

Liquefaction had removed the underlying soil of the roadway, depositing it into the ravine below.

"We need to find a way around this," said Paul, applying the emergency brake.

He opened the door and stepped onto the road to peer down into the darkness.

Tom and Angeline joined him, the light beams of the Jeep cutting the night like lasers. The darkness revealed little detail of the void, the chasm spanning at least fifteen feet. The only firm soil was to the extreme right, against the steep embankment. The paving was still intact on that side but the subsoil was questionable. The firm soil appeared to extend outwards for five feet before it inclined sharply into the ravine.

They would have to risk this precarious passage, the alternative being to abandon the Jeep and head for Port Albemi on foot.

Paul scratched his head. "This looks bad."

"There are two ways we can do this," Tom ventured, raising his voice above the noise of the Jeep's engine.

"We back up and rush it with the hope that the momentum will prevent a slide into the chasm, or we can inch over it very slowly, relying on traction and support at the foot of the embankment. It will also be possible to use the winch as a stabilizer."

"Good idea, Tom. I've used the winch only once—to pull my ATV out of the mud when camping with Meg and the kids last year. Never thought I'd be using it to drive over a ravine."

Tom grabbed the winch hook as Paul activated the release and looked for a suitable anchor on the other side of the landslide.

"That tree up there looks sturdy enough," shouted Paul.

He pointed to a large Douglas fir about twenty yards on. After a difficult but short climb, Tom attached the cable to the base.

"Keep an eye on the cable and the tree, Tom. I'm giving it a go."

Angeline placed her hand on Paul's arm. "Please, be careful."

Paul gunned the motor and began to inch his way across. Angeline watched from a safe distance, her heart in her throat, as she contemplated the possibilities.

The electronic winch slowly pulled the vehicle. There were hair-raising moments as the back wheels began to sink and the vehicle slipped sideways. Paul controlled his rising panic and eased off the accelerator. They all breathed a sigh of relief as the back wheels finally cleared the danger area and the Jeep was safely on stable ground.

"I thought for a moment you might end up in the ravine," Tom said as he and Angeline climbed back onboard.

"Piece of cake," Paul answered nonchalantly.

Being higher up in the pass, the air was colder so Paul cranked the heater up. Periodic gusts of wind rocked the Jeep as they pressed on. A stretch of badly damaged road appeared, and for the next hour, their progress slowed. Paul, in exasperation, decided it would be better to stop and wait until the morning. He pulled off the road to park for the night.

"What about the Irishman? What if he is still on our trail?" Angeline asked, her hands gripping the back of Tom's headrest.

Paul flipped on the interior light and pulled out an area map from the glove compartment.

"Have a look and see if you can estimate where we are at the moment, Tom."

Tom unfolded the map and searched for the Port Alberni/Tofino road.

"We're about thirty miles from Port Alberni. If we wait out the night, we would lose valuable time. Our families might need us," Tom replied.

Paul nodded. "If we keep going with this low visibility we could also fall into a ravine. I doubt if O'Kelly has been able to get across that last subsidence. I suggest we stop here for the night. We can take turns and keep watch just in case."

Tom thought for a moment and then agreed. "I guess the disaster response units will be looking after our families and travel on this road in the twilight could prove to be very dangerous."

Paul turned to Angeline. "There are two sleeping bags, several blankets and a small tent behind the backseat. Could you unpack them while Tom and I search for a spot to make camp? We'll bed down here for the night."

Angeline was glad to have something to do. It took her mind off the problems confronting them.

What really concerned Paul was the fact that Angeline would be alone in the tent with him and there was no telling where that might lead.

He had felt an increasing desire to put his arms around her and hold her close and caress her smooth, silky skin. He sensed she was attracted to him by the way she held his gaze when they spoke and the way she smiled when he looked at her. These signs conveyed more than words could tell.

Hours of grueling concentration were behind them and they suddenly realized that little thought had been given to families and life in Victoria. Their flight from the potential danger of the tsunami had been so intense that it had pushed their thoughts of home into the background.

While Tom and Angeline were setting up the tent, Paul used his cell phone to contact his family but there was no response. He tried again just to make sure the number had been entered correctly but still no answer. Tom's home number and that of the Geoscience Centre also produced no response.

After ten minutes, Paul tucked the phone into his pocket and walked to the tent-site with a worried frown on his forehead. A multitude of questions jeered malevolently at him. Was his family safe? The phone was the only way he could get answers but the quake might have destroyed all standard telecommunication.

"Make contact with anyone?" Tom asked.

"No—no response from anyone."

Angeline moved closer to Paul and said, "There's a strong possibility the phone system is suffering an overload. Everyone will be trying to use it at the same time."

"You are right. It's usually only the pay phones that work after an earthquake," he concluded.

Their arms touched and in the moonlight he could see the hint of a smile on her face.

Nine

O'Kelly and Banville.
Monday, 7:25 p.m. 25th September.

O'Kelly and Banville finally managed to conquer the embankment that kept them from apprehending the occupants of the Jeep. Their vehicle had not fared well in producing the required traction distribution for its wheels in the muddy soil.

They slithered backwards, slewed sideways and the back wheels sunk into the mud until, in sheer frustration, they gathered broken branches with leaves, to firm up the soil.

The two men were finally on their way, hoping to close in on the Jeep again.

"There'll probably be a few more landslides and obstacles that will slow them down and hopefully stop them," growled O'Kelly as he wrenched the steering wheel left and right to avoid patches of broken paving and fallen rocks.

"Yeah," Banville retorted, gently rubbing his swollen jaw. "I gotta bone to pick with that Brinkworth. He caught me by surprise, but it won't happen again."

Another hour passed without further conversation, until O'Kelly suddenly spotted the huge chasm in the road.

With the sound of tortured tires and showering gravel they came to a halt with the front wheels of the vehicle inches from the drop. O'Kelly cursed and hit the steering wheel several times with the palm of his hand. Resting his forehead on his muddy knuckles, he sighed in exasperation.

Banville rolled down his window. "They must have made it across."

"That means we can get across," O'Kelly said.

Banville got out to look around and immediately spotted the area next to the embankment where the landslide had been partially cleared.

The wind started to pick up, whistling around his ears as he peered across the crumbling soil at the formidable path ahead.

"I need to get ahold of Rushmore," said O'Kelly taking out his cell phone. To his chagrin there was no signal.

Banville said, "I doubt there will be any reception here in the mountains. I think I know what Rushmore would say, though—eliminate the threat!"

O'Kelly shot Banville an annoyed glance. "I know that but he needs to know what's happened. We'll have to take a chance on the incline next to the embankment."

The two men inspected the potential crossing area. The only other option would be to abandon the vehicle and continue on foot.

"It doesn't look as though they had too much trouble, but those Jeeps are pretty good—they can go anywhere," said O' Kelly, scratching his head.

"We should collect a few rocks and place them in the soil on the edge. It may help compact the loose stuff and give us extra traction," Banville added.

"Good idea. We want to get over this as quickly as possible."

For the next fifteen minutes both men collected all the small rocks they could find and packed them in the soft soil on the edge of the firm ground next to the embankment.

O'Kelly instructed Banville to wait on the other side while he backed up in readiness for the crossing. His idea was to pick up speed and allow the momentum of the vehicle to carry it over the dangerous area—exactly the opposite of what Paul had decided. He released the emergency brake and then stuck his hand out the window to signal Banville to stand aside.

After a last look at the dark void falling away to his left, O'Kelly fixed his eyes on the area ahead and pressed the accelerator to the floor. The motor bellowed at peak revs as the vehicle hit the danger area. Barely touching the ground it reached the firm soil on the other side without mishap, coming to a standstill about thirty yards up the road. With a sigh of relief Banville clambered onboard, more eager than ever, to catch up with their quarry.

The same bad patches of roadway that had hindered the progress of the first vehicle now imposed itself on the second and the two men struggled on as fast as the terrain would allow.

Eventually in the distance, at the extremity of the headlight beams, they saw the back reflectors of Paul's stationary vehicle. Excitement of the anticipated confrontation gripped them.

O'Kelly drove up to within fifty yards of the Jeep and stopped. With relish he pulled out the revolver, turned to Banville and grinned.

"Let's get 'em."

They strode off confidently toward the Jeep, not bothering to hide their approach.

**

Monday, 9:00 p.m. 25th September.

The Saanich Peninsula Hospital was experiencing the worst crisis in its history. Due to a lack of doctors and trained staff it had become difficult to deal with the influx of casualties that continued to flow in from the disaster torn neighborhood.

One of the two doctors who had made it to the hospital was examining a patient. "Megan Brinkworth, thirty-five years of age...head injury...severe concussion and possible skull fracture," he read aloud from the chart hung at the end of the bed.

He placed his hand beneath the dark curls of Meg's hair to gently feel the area of the suspected fracture. With a worried look at the nurse he felt for the pulse and checked the chart again.

"Her pulse is getting weaker and there is a definite sign of a subdural hematoma. Shave a patch on this side of the head—we'll have to release the pressure on the brain. We have to find someone to look at the back-up power system before we risk operating."

Paul's mother Lillian, Amy and Jason, waited impatiently in the upstairs reception for the surgery to take place. Lillian was not coping well. She watched her granddaughter sitting on the sofa opposite her, subdued to the point of helplessness and detachment. Her grandson, on the other hand, seemed unruffled by the calamity and destruction, a sign that he had switched off and distanced himself from reality. How she wished her late husband was still there to see how his grandchildren had grown—he would be so proud, she thought.

Earlier, Amy had called from a pay phone at the hospital reception to let her grandmother know about the accident. Lillian, throwing all caution to the wind about the road conditions, had raced off to pick up Jason alone at home and then to the hospital to join her granddaughter.

She could hardly believe the sudden turn of events. In the space of a few minutes a contented family had been devastated and their world turned upside down. She tried to contemplate the answers to the questions Amy and Jason were asking. Where was their father and would they see him again? Would their mother recover and if not, how would they survive without parents?

The three family members waited patiently on a bench in the waiting room. The hallway that led to the surgery was a cacophony of noise. People milled about and peered with anxious faces into the various wards. Nurses scurried backward and forward with harrowed looks on their faces, trying to look as calm as possible, avoiding eye contact.

In Amy's mind the double doors of the surgery seemed larger than normal. They represented the entrance to an austere world with unimaginable scientific and medical mystery.

She knew the product of the efforts beyond those doors would bring forth uncertain news. She stared at the doors in anticipation of the surgeon's appearance, willing him to bring good tidings.

Engrossed in thought she failed to see a man approaching and only noticed him when he sat next to her. He touched her knee lightly in a greeting.

"Hi, Amy—I came to see how your mom's doing."

As she turned to look at him, a deep blush crept up from her throat and her heart quickened as he put his arm around her shoulders and gave her a little squeeze.

Lillian looked startled and was about to say something to the young man when Amy spoke. "Grandma, this is Dan. He's the one who rescued Mom and I from the wreck."

Lillian's face lit up as she extended her hand to Dan Duplessis and verbalized her gratefulness for the heroic rescue. He blushed modestly under the accolade and assured he was only doing his job.

They chatted amiably for several minutes about the work that the DART teams were involved in, then the double doors of the surgery burst open and the surgeon emerged. He stood with hands on hips and mask dangling around his neck, searching the faces of those in the waiting area.

Amy immediately jumped up and ran to him, her face expectant and questioning. "Is my mom okay?"

The others gathered around quickly to hear what he had to say. "Your mother has suffered a very dangerous hematoma brought on by a severe blow to the head. There was a lot of bleeding which placed pressure on the brain—we had to operate to relieve the pressure.

"Unfortunately the back-up power system has not been very kind, failing on us toward the end, but I'm happy to say the procedure appears to have been successful."

The news was encouraging and after a few more questions they waited for Megan to be transported from surgery to the recovery room, where they lingered around her bed.

Her head was swathed in post-operative bandages, her face pale and drawn. Amy buried her face in her hands and sobbed, overwhelmed by all that had happened.

Dan put his arm around her shoulder and gently whispered what consolations he could think of while a nurse busied herself checking Meg's vital signs. Her body language made it clear it was time for all of them to leave.

They quietly left, walking slowly to the entrance foyer, reluctant to depart without Meg. Dan took a card out of his wallet and handed it to Lillian.

"If you need help with anything please give me a call. My cell phone's working and you should be able to get ahold of me for the next couple of days, but after that, it's difficult to say...depends on whether the DART teams are required to help out in other areas on the island."

A nurse came running up to them and spoke briefly to Lillian. "I found this cell phone in Mrs. Brinkworth's jacket pocket—best take it home with you and bring it back when she has recovered."

Lillian looked at the phone and gave it to Amy.

"You know I'm way behind on all this technology and being so absent minded I may forget where I put it."

Amy smiled and said, "No problem, Grandma, I'll take care of it."

They said their goodbyes to Dan and left the hospital.

**

Monday, 9:10 p.m. 25th September.

The moon cast its silvery sheen across the mountains, creating an illusion of peace.

Yet, all was not peaceful—the atmosphere was charged with tension and expectancy.

After Tom and Angeline had pitched the tent, Paul made a fire to brew much needed coffee. They sat around the coals, warming themselves and lamenting the day's disaster.

Several more attempts at contacting each home were made using Paul's cell phone, but to no avail. He knew it would be fruitless to contact 911 because they would have their hands full for a few days.

The most sensible thing to do was head for Port Alberni and refuel the Jeep. The gas tank was below one quarter full. From there they could make their way down to Nanaimo and then Victoria depending on the negotiability of the Malahat Pass.

Tom took the first watch and stretched out on the backseat of the Jeep.

Paul and Angeline crawled into the tent on hands and knees to roll out the sleeping bags. The ground was hard and cold but the bags were warm. All was quiet.

They settled down, both acutely aware, that for the first time they were entirely alone. For the next few hours their dreams and fantasies would drive them unrelentingly toward each other.

Paul tried to shift his thoughts to his wife and children but another force, the close presence of this lovely, young woman compelled him to push family considerations to the back of his mind. He felt like a teenager approaching his first conquest.

"You tired, Angie?"

"It's been a long and hectic day—my body is tired and my mind's going in circles. What are you thinking about, Paul?"

"Lots of things. My family in particular."

"What else are you thinking about?" she ventured solicitously.

"You and me together—alone in this tent." Paul flinched as he said it.

He was lying on his back with his head turned towards her, trying to make out her form in the gloom. She lay with her back toward him, her face turned slightly upward.

Sensing his probing thoughts she turned toward him and he reached out to her, drawing her close. A moment later Paul thought he heard a vehicle approaching their camp.

"What's that? Angeline asked.

"It sounded like a truck."

"Do you think it could be O'Kelly?" she asked nervously.

"I'm not sure—it's possible."

*

Tom watched the vehicle approach before the driver pulled onto the verge and stopped. Opening the back door of the Jeep, Tom whistled softly in the direction of the tent, hoping to attract Paul's attention without having to use his voice. When Paul did not respond immediately he called, cupping one hand to the side of his mouth, keeping his voice as calm as he could. He called twice before Paul responded.

"What's happening, Tom?"

"We've got company. I'm sure it's that O'Kelly fellow and he has someone with him."

135

Paul cursed softly and ducked back into the tent to pull on his jacket and boots. Angeline looked up at him in alarm. Already halfway out of her sleeping bag, she murmured, "What's happening?"

"Don't be frightened, Angie, we'll be all right. I want you to take my cell phone and flashlight. Hide up on the ridge somewhere. I'll whistle when it's safe to come back."

Angeline extracted herself from the sleeping bag and without question she scurried out of the tent and up the incline toward the ridge above them. There was enough moonlight to see reasonably clearly.

She half scrambled and climbed until some distance was placed between her and the campsite.

Paul and Tom stood next to the Jeep and waited for the two men to reach them. Paul hoped they would be able to avoid a confrontation but as he watched their menacing approach, he realized there would be no easy bargains.

Sporting a satisfied smirk, O'Kelly spoke. "Well, well, well— what do we have here? Did you think you could get away from us that easily?"

"We don't know what you're getting at, O'Kelly. We don't know what you fellows are up to in the forest, but my guess is its illegal. I'm warning you that any attempt to silence us will not work. There are people who know we came up here today and if any harm comes to us you'll pay for it!"

O'Kelly found Paul's answer amusing. He grinned accommodatingly and turned to Banville. "They're rattled aren't they?"

Banville grinned and fingered his injured jaw. He stared at Paul. "You and I have a fucking score to settle."

Paul ignored Banville, addressing his next words to O'Kelly. "What is Hurricane Charlie?"

O'Kelly's eyes narrowed.

"Don't you be questioning what we're doing. And what's more, you're under a gross misconception if you think anyone would be worrying about you after the earthquake—they'll be taking care of themselves first."

Paul knew O'Kelly had a point and it would not be any use threatening them with the sudden appearance of the law.

"What do you intend to do with us?" interjected Tom, trying to look much taller than his five foot eight inches.

O'Kelly ignored his question. Turning to his companion he snapped, "Look in the tent and bring the girl out. At least we can have some fun before we dispose of these two assholes."

He waved the gun threateningly in Paul's direction, guessing that going after Angeline would evoke Paul's anger.

"Don't even think of touching her!" Paul took a step forward. Tom immediately restrained his friend, grabbing his arm, afraid that O'Kelly would shoot him.

Banville expectantly peered into the tent. He looked at Paul and snarled, "Where's your little girl?"

Paul's mind scrambled for a story that would discourage them from looking for Angeline.

"When we ran out of gas we decided to camp here for the night but the woman and our other friend felt they could make Port Alberni on foot. They've gone to get help," he lied.

"Why would the woman go instead of one of you?" questioned O'Kelly suspiciously.

Tom answered this time, very convincingly. "She left one of her kids with relatives in Alberni and nothing we said could stop her from getting back there."

O'Kelly walked to the tent and looked inside. Seeing the two sleeping bags, he shook his head angrily and glared at the two men.

"She's around here somewhere. You're both lying through your teeth!"

Again he snapped an order at Banville, instructing him to bring their vehicle up to the camp so they could transfer the gas to the Jeep's fuel tank.

"You won't be needing your vehicle any longer so you might as well hand over the keys. Now, where's the girl?"

"We told you—she's walked off with the fourth member of our party."

"I remember seeing only three of you," O'Kelly said irritably.

"The fourth person was behind us in the forest when the earthquake hit."

"I don't have time for these fucking games, Brinkworth! Forget about the girl. We are taking your vehicle."

Tom lifted his chin and looked at O'Kelly. "That's theft!"

O'Kelly laughed. "Call it what you like."

Angeline watched from her hiding place on the ridge above, her heart pounding, as O'Kelly, standing behind Paul, raised the revolver and aimed at Paul's head. She froze and wanted to retch but managed to suppress it. O'Kelly stood motionless for endless seconds before raising the gun and bringing the butt down hard on the back of Paul's head.

∞

Ten

Tom and Paul Take Action.
Monday, 9:15 p.m. 25th September.

Paul was momentarily stunned by the blow from the butt of O'Kelly's revolver. Tom gaped in horror at O'Kelly, expecting to receive the same treatment, but O'Kelly ignored him and barked an order at Banville.

"Bring our vehicle and park it next Brinkworth's Jeep. We need to transfer the gas from the Land Cruiser."

Banville trotted off to where they left their vehicle while O'Kelly waited, the revolver pointed in the general direction of his two prisoners. Tom moved slowly over to Paul's inert form, wanting to see if his friend was all right but O'Kelly warned him off.

"Keep away from him. He'll survive—for now."

Tom shrank back and sat on his haunches. Eventually Banville arrived with the Land Cruiser and backed it up to the rear of the Jeep.

"I'll look for something we can use to siphon gas," he shouted to O'Kelly.

There was a mess of empty plastic bottles and empty take-out cups in the back of the Land

Cruiser. Banville quickly discovered a small container of gas hidden under an old towel, holding about one gallon of fuel and a short plastic hose.

"Now we can make some headway," he commented to O'Kelly and proceeded to drain the remnants of the Land Cruiser's tank into the container.

Earlier, Paul had reluctantly handed over the Jeep's keys to O'Kelly, when requested. There appeared to be little alternative to submission while a revolver was pointed at his head. They were O'Kelly's prisoners and there was nothing he could do about it.

After a few more minutes Paul regained full consciousness and sat up holding his head in his hands. Pain shot down his neck and into his shoulders causing him to groan slightly as he tried to clear his mind. Tom looked at him with concern. "Are you okay, Paul?"

Paul glared at O'Kelly and answered. "Yeah, I'm a little shook up but I'll be all right."

O'Kelly grinned broadly and said, "There'll be more of that if I have any problem with you, Brinkworth."

Paul stared malevolently at him but said nothing. Banville continued the syphoning process, stopping every now and then to spit out gas-tainted saliva and the container was close to full. He had stopped syphoning for a second to check the container when they felt a vibration under their feet—slight at first but gaining in intensity, until everything around them was jumping and shaking. It only lasted ten seconds but Paul couldn't have been happier as to its timing.

The aftershock was huge, almost as bad as a second quake and it dislodged loose rocks on the ridge that came raining down, taking O'Kelly and Banville completely by surprise.

Paul did not wait. As the intensity of the aftershock increased he launched himself at O'Kelly, who had been struck heavily by rocks from the ridge above. The two men grappled, falling to the ground.

The revolver was still clutched in the Irishman's hand. They rolled over and over but Paul being bigger and stronger quickly overpowered O'Kelly and delivered a crunching blow to his jaw.

Tom had tackled the bigger and more powerful Banville, but was not faring as well as his friend. Banville had managed to roll on top of Tom and was busy pounding the lecturer's face. Paul, having downed O'Kelly, caught Banville from behind with a powerful headlock and twisted him around, cutting off his air supply. As strong as Banville was, he couldn't break Paul's hold and finally succumbed to lack of oxygen.

O'Kelly lay spread-eagled on the ground, his face turned up toward the moonlit sky. The revolver was nowhere to be seen.

Paul, still feeling the effects of the earlier blow to his head, helped Tom to his feet. "Did you see what happened to his gun?"

Tom, visibly shaken answered, "No, it could be under loose rocks. Thanks for coming to my aid."

"You're welcome—let's find that gun," Paul responded, a little winded by his efforts.

They both searched the rock-strewn ground for the revolver but could not find it. Finally, Paul remembered that Angeline was somewhere on the embankment and he called out to her.

She came stumbling down the incline and fell into his arms, on the verge of hysteria and was unable to get her words out coherently. Her voice was hoarse and shaky and the tears came like a flood. "I thought they were going to shoot you."

At that moment Tom sensed a movement behind him and on turning saw O'Kelly had regained consciousness and was pulling the gun from behind his back. Tom hissed a warning and there was a small red flame, accompanied by a white puff of smoke, as the gun discharged its package of death.

Paul threw Angeline to the ground and jerked sideways as the bullet passed through the cloth of his jacket, creasing his right arm.

Without thinking Tom threw himself at O'Kelly, who was about to take another shot at Paul. He heard the revolver discharge a second time and felt the crunch of the bullet as it hit him in the chest. A burning pain engulfed him, followed by numbness in his arms and legs.

A peace filtered through his thoughts and his feet were no longer touching the ground. He was flying through a beautiful, cerulean sky that yielded brilliant halogen stars. Images from the past came to greet him, floating into view like friendly clouds on a warm summer's day.

He fell at O'Kelly's feet and rolled onto his side, his eyes staring blankly at the heavens.

Paul had already started his rush forward and was on top of O'Kelly before he could fire the third shot, his hands grasping for the Irishman's scrawny throat. The full weight of Paul's body caught O'Kelly across the chest, pinning him to the ground, forcing the air out of his lungs.

For what seemed like an eternity Paul shook the man's head, banging it against the ground, his hands clenching O'Kelly's throat in a vice-like grip, intent on driving the life out of the man's body.

Angeline grabbed Paul by the arm and screamed. "Paul! Stop! You'll kill him."

Paul took no notice at first but after a full minute had passed, he regained his sanity and released his grip.

O'Kelly's body was as limp as a ragdoll's and the Irishman appeared to be dead, his eyes staring sightlessly and mouth hanging open.

Paul turned to Tom and lifted his friend into a sitting position, holding the still form against his own body, calling his name again and again, without response. After a few minutes he realized that his friend would not be revived—Tom was dead.

**

Monday, 9:52 p.m. 25th September.

Paul and Angeline wrapped Tom's body in the tent, taking care to tie it well to avoid exposure to the elements.

Angeline was silent, her face pale and tear stained. Paul glanced at O'Kelly's body and said, "When does this nightmare end?"

Angeline glanced at him but said nothing.

Banville had regained consciousness and was sitting quietly next to O'Kelly's still form. Paul had the revolver tucked into his belt so it was visible but did not expect any trouble from Banville.

They did not know if O'Kelly was still alive and neither did they care. It was enough to go about the business of saying goodbye to their friend and securing his body, without the thought of having to bother with two thugs.

Paul decided it would be better to leave the body and return for it later as they did not know what lay ahead of them.

Banville appeared to respect their need to grieve and if he was concerned about O'Kelly he did not show it. He just sat there, looking solemnly at the ground, ignoring Paul and Angeline.

Paul suggested they collect as many small rocks as possible to place them on top of the body, thus forming a protective barrier against predators. He that remembered bears and cougars roamed freely on parts of the island and the body would not be safe if left lying in the open.

When they had completed the make-shift grave, he packed the sleeping bags into the Jeep, called Angeline, and without saying a word to Banville, they drove away.

The journey forward was undertaken in silence. The reality of Tom's death sank in and the strain of grief was visible on their faces.

Paul glanced quickly at the dash clock as he guided the Jeep around the occasional crevice and crack in the road surface. The McKenzie Mountains, languishing in the moon's glow, towered above them like giant sentinels on an eternal vigil.

**

Monday evening. Quake aftermath. 25th September.

Bud Hamlin scrambled to the safety of his vehicle as the first aftershock shook the already devastated island to its core. Buildings that had been severely damaged collapsed in heaps of wood and masonry.

The thundering roar intermingled with screams of terror. Clouds of dust, unseen in the night sky, billowed high into the atmosphere and red, angry flames lit the street in various places.

Bud had been surveying the catastrophic position of the waterfront in front of the famous Empress Hotel, where the Queen of England had stayed on colonial visits. The grass lawns of the Empress and a section of Government Street were awash in the waters of James Bay.

That meant the entire waterfront area, all the way to the east side of the island, could be under water. He was standing at the water's edge, contemplating the consequences of the sinking island when the aftershock arrived.

A section of collapsing building thundered down next to his vehicle, engulfing the immediate area in dust and flying debris. When the dust had settled he cracked the window slightly open. There were cries of alarm coming from several areas close by. *People trapped by fallen debris or just frightened by the aftershock,* he thought pensively.

Bud realized there was nothing he could do to help the injured. He had a job to do and that was to direct the emergency response of the many organizations involved in the rescue of the island's inhabitants. While this sobering thought shot fleetingly through his mind, the radio crackled to life.

"Come in, Bud," shouted Raymond Boyd.

"Read you, Ray," Hamlin answered calmly.

"Just to let you know—all the D.A.R.T members, bar one, have managed to mobilize."

"Have you had any reports on suburban casualties yet?" asked Bud.

"One of the team leaders reported a bad accident off Route 17. The driver of an eighteen wheeler crushed an SUV. There appears to have been one fatality."

"Any reports on the condition of houses in general?"

"Most of the homes have suffered minor structural damage."

"Remind your guys to gather as much info on the damage as possible," advised Hamlin, knowing when the news reports were sent out, the world would want to know all the details.

"Will do, Bud."

"Thanks, Ray. Keep me posted," Hamlin concluded.

Bud changed frequency. He needed to find out how the emergency reception areas in each community were faring.

"ERC 1, come in, please." The radio crackled.

"ERC 1, Dianne here."

"Dianne, this is Bud Hamlin. What's the status?"

"The emergency workers have all arrived and we are fully operational, over."

"Any deaths, or injuries?"

"Not many in this area, Bud. Most people are just hungry and frightened."

"There are likely to be more aftershocks so be prepared. Do you have adequate drinking water and food?"

"Yes, our supplies have arrived."

There were ten emergency reception centers set up in schools to help those requiring minor first aid, food, and drinking water. The speed of their mobilization would alleviate much hardship and suffering.

He was gratified that the first center he had contacted was already operational. There was so much to be done.

**

Monday, 10:05 p.m. 25th September.

The bright moonlight bathed the mountains in a soft glow under the cloudless sky.

Andre Banville sat passively on the ground next to his fallen comrade, rubbing a painful neck, still hurting from the tangle with Paul Brinkworth. His neck was not the greatest of his present problems however, as the man lying next to him, looked awfully dead.

O'Kelly was the local agent for an international drug smuggling syndicate, the details of which Banville knew little about.

O'Kelly had always been secretive about the hierarchy he reported to, keeping Banville at arm's length. The only other person he really knew was Hilda, who appeared to be a courier of some sort and he wasn't even sure where she lived. Brinkworth would blow the whistle on the rainforest lab operation the moment he reached the local R.C.M.P offices in Port Alberni—there was little he could do about anything. The only hope was the delay the local authorities would experience in the aftermath of the quake. He could just walk away and disappear from the scene, leaving O'Kelly's body to its fate.

Banville had never personally had anything to do with the local planning of the operation. It was Sean O'Kelly's responsibility to plan the weekly quotas and see they were packaged for transport to a warehouse in Nanaimo. Hilda, whom he saw occasionally, arrived every Sunday to pick up the packages from the lab.

O'Kelly had offered Banville good money to assist in the manufacturing of Canada's latest craze— Hurricane Charley. Hurricane Charley, more commonly known as Bath Salts, was an extremely dangerous drug.

The rainforest was the perfect place for such an operation, providing invisibility for the production facility. A senior official in the parks board had made the opportunity possible by turning a blind eye for a stake in the profits.

Banville felt a strange detachment from the scene that surrounded him. He did not want to think about his next move but a strong notion of making an escape was high on his priority list.

It was possible for him to leave the island for the United States where his brother lived. It seemed a viable course of action to escape retribution and imprisonment by the Canadian authorities.

In deep contemplation of his uncertain future, he was unaware of the slight movement from the body lying next to him. A groan rattled in O'Kelly's throat. He was still alive.

O'Kelly's face looked hideous in the bright moonlight. His nose had been broken and blood was congealing on his cheeks. Banville lurched into motion and knelt next to the Irishman, taking the battered face in his hands.

"Sean? Can you hear me?" he called several times into O'Kelly's ear.

O'Kelly opened his eyes and coughed several times. It took a few minutes before he could sit upright with Banville's help. Banville had found a water bottle in the truck and was gently applying a wet cloth to the Irishman's broken nose.

Eventually O'Kelly spoke. "How long ago did they leave?"

"About ninety minutes. They took the Jeep and the remaining gas so we can't use the Land Cruiser."

"What happened to the guy I shot?" O'Kelly's voice sounded like a rasp on tough metal.

"He's over there, wrapped in their tent, under all those stones. He's dead."

"Well, that settles it then," O'Kelly muttered. "We have to get word to Hilda as quickly as possible. Brinkworth and his girlfriend must be stopped. We have to get to Port Alberni—maybe the phone system's working."

"It's at least fourteen miles to that settlement outside Sprout Lake. If you're up to it we can set out straight away and maybe get there by morning," Andre added hopefully.

O'Kelly shrugged. "Doesn't matter how I feel. We have work to do. Maybe we can find a useable vehicle when we get there and drive the rest of the way to Alberni."

Banville helped him to his feet. "At least we have some water."

O'Kelly felt his strength returning. "Let's get moving, time is of the essence." O'Kelly felt a new surge of energy flooding into his body, fired by the most dangerous of all emotions—hate

∞

Eleven

Alone in the Mountains.
Tuesday, 5:12 a.m. 26th September.

Paul awoke with a start. For a brief moment he felt disorientated but then the events of the previous day came flooding back to him. The first light of dawn was sneaking across the sky as he turned to look at Angeline, huddled in her sleeping bag next to him. Her lips were slightly parted and the cadence of her breath was slow and rhythmic. He watched for some time, admiring the peaceful look on her face and enjoyed the moment of solitude.

Soon the rising sun would cut through the tall Douglas Firs bringing warmth to the coolness of the Jeep's interior. Propping himself up on his elbows Paul tried to look out of the back window but heavy condensation on the glass prevented him from seeing anything outside. He turned to look at Angeline again.

She appeared to be in a deep sleep. Her soft, blond hair lay across her shoulder as if a hairdresser had carefully arranged it. He became more aware of how outrageously beautiful she was and felt enormously flattered that she had found him attractive. Again he sensed the struggle with his integrity.

He closed his eyes in an effort to dispel the guilt. When he opened them, he was looking into two pools of exquisite blue that captivated and drew him irresistibly to their warmth.

He reached out his hand to touch her face, the smooth, silky skin of her cheek was like velvet. For the moment, the earthquake and all its devastation was forgotten. He leaned forward and kissed her lips gently.

Her response was immediate and hungry, without reservation. They unzipped their sleeping bags and moved toward each other with eagerness and commitment, caressing, stroking, evoking that sensual passion, born of sudden intimacy.

All thoughts of previous loss, the devastation of the quake and their dire predicament, were completely engulfed—lost in a tidal wave of desire. This moment belonged to them and they would live it with urgency.

Later that morning, Paul busied himself with the gathering of firewood, for a breakfast fire. Angeline found a way to a stream that cut below the road. It was cool and she shivered as she washed her face in the icy mountain water, enjoying the fresh tingling sensation on her skin.

There had been no time to retrieve the overnight bag from her car before their rush for safety from the tsunami. She would just have to survive with the clothes she was wearing.

Despite the violence and tragedy of the preceding day, Angeline felt a stirring she had not felt for some time. It was the same feeling she had when she first made love to her ex-husband. Unfortunately, the marriage ended in divorce three years later.

Paul walked to the verge of the road to see where Angeline had gone. She did not see him gazing down at her, contemplating her loveliness.

He softly called her name. She turned and then rose quickly to clamber up the steep slope like a happy teenage girl on a picnic, into his waiting arms. They stood there kissing and caressing each other for several minutes until he said, "Feel like something to eat?"

"We have food?" she asked with a smile.

"Emergency rations from my earthquake kit. The fire is made and the water should be boiling by now."

After breakfast Paul inspected the mass of rock and rubble that blocked their way. It seemed the only option available was to leave the vehicle and climb over the top of the slide. This meant a long hike down the highway to Port Alberni. He desperately needed to get back to Victoria before the day was done. This would obviously be impossible without the Jeep.

An idea that appeared totally impossible kept tumbling around in his head. It was so dangerous that at first he discounted it, but the more he thought about it, the greater became the determination to try it. He decided to share the idea with Angeline.

"I think I know how we can get the Jeep out of here." Angeline stared at him incredulously.

He looked thoughtfully at the mountain that towered over them and pointed to a place just above the slide.

"Do you see that tree? Remember how we managed to cross the last obstacle by using the winch? That's how we can do it."

Angeline stared at the tree but remained silent.

"I know it's dangerous but it's also feasible and possible," he stated. "We need the vehicle and I'm sure that once we're clear of the mountains, the going will be a lot easier."

Angeline reacted negatively, "l think it will be far too dangerous. What if the tree becomes uprooted or the winch cable brakes? You and the Jeep will end up in the bottom of the ravine."

"I think it makes sense to try. I'm going to climb up and see what's on the other side—are you coming?" Paul had already made the decision.

He retrieved the coil of repel rope he kept next to the spare wheel. She sat looking at him for a few moments, then with a shake of her head, followed him to the vehicle.

He climbed to the top of the rock pile and surveyed the area on the other side where the road appeared to be free of any further obstacles. He judged the tree to be well situated for the purpose, almost in the center and about ten feet above the top of the pile, which would allow space for the winch to pull the Jeep up the steep incline. Once on top of the mound of rock and soil, he would maneuver the Jeep, then slowly winch it backwards, down the opposite slope to level ground.

He checked the base of the tree and it appeared to be firmly rooted. Angeline stood below him, her arms folded, looking doubtful.

"Do you really think the winch can pull the weight?"

"Not totally, but the wheels will have enough traction to reduce the actual dead weight."

She was not convinced. "How will that work?"

"I will keep the four-wheel drive operating as the winch pulls."

"I'm afraid, Paul," she lamented softly.

"I'm also scared, but I think it will work."

He fastened the rope to the tree then rappelled to the road.

"I will tie everything together—the sleeping bags and the supplies—then secure them to my belt. Now that I have the rope it will be easier to get back to the top of the slide again."

"Why don't you just leave everything in the Jeep?" asked Angeline.

"I think it would be better to keep these items out of the vehicle in case something goes wrong and I end up in the ravine below."

She was unhappy with the plan. "The winch cable may not be strong enough to hold the weight."

Paul attempted to put her at ease. "The half-inch thick cable should be capable of handling the Jeep's total dead weight."

She finally breathed a sigh of acceptance and moved close to him as he inspected the winch, putting her arms around his neck.

"It all looks so overwhelmingly impossible," she murmured plaintively. He held her close for a moment and then released her.

"I need to secure the winch—I don't know how long this will take, so we had better get moving."

Paul hoisted the cable and their supplies to the top of the rockslide. He wound the winch cable around the tree several times and tested it with his own weight to make sure it was well secured.

Angeline, still standing below the rockslide, called to him. "How are you going to turn the Jeep around up there?"

"I'll leave the cable attached and use the four-wheel drive to maneuver backwards and forwards until I'm facing the other way. There's limited space on top of the mound but the slope isn't as steep. Providing the wheels can find enough purchase, I can do it."

He was so determined that she declined to make any more comments. They embraced, holding each other tightly for a long moment, then without further talk he pointed to the rope and she meekly obeyed.

When she had pulled herself to the top of the rock pile, he sat in the driver's seat, staring up at the tree, praying it would take the weight. Then turning the ignition key he started the engine, at the same time shifting into the lower four-wheel drive provision. With the flick of a switch he put the winch into motion and braced himself.

The incline in front of him was not vertical but close. The height of the rock pile was fifteen yards, a formidable distance for the battery-operated winch to pull such a heavy load with limited assistance from the drive train.

Paul figured with the incline there would be sufficient weight on the wheels to give some purchase on the rock face. The going would become more difficult in the looser rocks and soil above the solid rock surface. At that point the gradient started to decrease which would result in more weight being placed on the wheels—at least in theory.

He shifted into low gear and let the engine idle along as the winch began to pull the nose of the Jeep upwards, scraping the winch housing against the inclining rock.

Eventually it was drawn clear and the Jeep was on its back wheels like a rearing stallion, clawing at the rock face. Paul kept his foot lightly on the gas, trying to judge the speed of the winch as it drew the vehicle into an almost vertical position. He kept the accelerator in that position until all four wheels were making contact with the rock surface. Under gravity, the weight of his body sank into the backrest and a few minutes later blue sky came into view through the windshield.

Perspiration poured from his brow as he concentrated on the winch speed and began to apply pressure on the accelerator. The wheels gained a certain amount of purchase and the Jeep moved slowly up the incline.

Angeline stood next to the tree, staring intently at Paul's face, looking for the slightest sign of panic. Everything seemed to be going fine and the Jeep was making slow but steady progress up the slope to the point where the gradient changed. Paul felt the tension beginning to ease and his breathing became easier. Then above the whine of the winch, and the smooth hum of the Jeep's engine, came a new noise.

He thought the front wheels had started to bite into loose rocks until he realized that everything around him, even the ground outside, was shaking. Rocks were pounding against the windshield and dust poured in through the window. He had a glimpse of Angeline clinging to the tree with rocks, soil, and dust flying everywhere. The island was enduring the second of many aftershocks to come.

Paul hung onto the steering wheel, desperately trying to force down the rising panic that threatened his ability to keep the drive train moving at a speed compatible with the winch.

The wheels bit into the softer surface as the incline decreased, causing the Jeep to lurch forward and then fall back again, placing tremendous strain on the cable. Smoke poured from the front of the vehicle as the winch clutch began to slip.

Panic stricken Paul stopped the winch motor, praying the vehicle would not slide backwards. He hit the Jeep's emergency brake and sat frozen, like a chameleon in mid stride.

With closed eyes he waited, bracing his body for the impending plunge into the ravine below. The noise of the shaking earth blocked out all other sound and the stench of his own fear mingled with the dust in his nostrils.

Finally the shuddering stopped and Paul opened his eyes to see the clear, early morning sky. Dust covered the windshield and a crack had appeared across his line of vision. He raised himself gingerly by pulling up on the steering wheel to see if Angeline was safe. To his relief she was still there, clinging to the tree.

"Are you okay, Angie?" he called to her, hoping she could hear. She waved, indicating she was unhurt. He felt a vibration through the back of his seat and realized the Jeep's engine was still running.

With his right foot hard on the brake pedal and the Jeep still in low gear, he wrestled with the thought of setting the winch into operation again. Slowly he released the emergency brake. If the clutch began to burn against the load he would have to leave the vehicle and they would be forced to take their chances.

Looking skyward he uttered a silent prayer and flicked the switch. There was an immediate response as the winch began to turn, slowly at first, before picking up momentum. He gently eased off the pressure on the brake pedal and simultaneously pressed down on the accelerator.

The front wheels started to dig down but the Quadra-track system came to the rescue, transferring the power to the back wheels.

Slowly the Jeep began to move forward until the back wheels hit the softer soil at which point the front wheels gained more traction. As the gradient lessened the winch began to pull the heavy load with greater ease.

Suddenly the winch was belching smoke again as the over-taxed clutch began to slip and Paul realized he had to transfer the forward progress totally to the wheel train.

Loose rocks shot out from under the wheels as he put his foot on the accelerator. The powerful V8 motor coped easily, bringing the Jeep to the summit without further incident.

With the vehicle on a more horizontal plane Paul turned the engine off before setting the emergency brake. He stepped out of the vehicle with a broad grin on his face. Angeline clambered down the small embankment that supported the tree and ran to him. They clung to each other, allowing the built-up tension to dissipate, before Paul broke the silence. "See, I told you—piece of cake!"

"I didn't think it possible, but you were right," she said happily.

The battle of the rock pile was by no means over. There was still the repositioning of the Jeep and the descent to the road on the other side.

He looked around the small area on which they stood. "I need rocks to act as markers."

They found and placed them in a semi-circle around the Jeep, marking off an area of safety, within which Paul would attempt to maneuver the vehicle. There was a safe zone of about seven square yards, precious little space in which to turn the vehicle around.

It took another five minutes to accomplish the one hundred and eighty-degree turn. The rear of the Jeep was finally facing the right direction with the winch secured to the tree again. This time the cable would only be used as a brake, while Paul negotiated the steepest part of the decline, backwards.

He climbed back into the driver's seat. "Time to make the descent."

With the Jeep's brakes fully engaged and the winch cable under tension, Paul slowly backed the vehicle down the slope toward level ground. Ten minutes later the Jeep was safely deposited on the road below. A relieved Angeline released the cable from the tree and hastily clambered down to the Jeep, using the repel rope.

Paul quickly inspected the Jeep's undercarriage for damage but all appeared to be in good order. Apart from scratch marks on the front bumper, a cracked windshield and lots of dust, the vehicle passed the test with flying colors. He glanced at his watch—7:40 a.m.

The emergency equipment and sleeping bags were loaded back into the vehicle and with a final farewell glance at the rock pile they set out to continue the journey.

*

Paul and Angeline reached Port Alberni before nine without any further incident. The road conditions had improved after the mountain pass was behind them and they had made good time. The sun's rays were peeping through the early morning mist as they entered Port Alberni.

Paul had consistently tried to contact Meg and Gertrude but the phones just continued to give a busy signal. He suddenly remembered a fact that he had recently read about phone service after an earthquake—because of the overload of calls being made by survivors and concerned citizens it was better to use texting. He had already sent texts to his wife and the director of the GSC but nothing was forthcoming.   Angeline had also tried to call her office, but to no avail.

The small town of Port Alberni was in chaos. All the buildings on the waterfront at the end of Johnston Road had been severely damaged by the tsunami as it surged up the Alberni inlet. Various smaller businesses situated along the Somas River had been washed away or lay in ruins under heaps of debris.

River Road was littered with rubble and the remains of once flourishing enterprises. In contrast, the suburbs did not appear to have suffered much.

People were busy helping to clear the road at the corner of River and Johnston. These were the first reconstructive efforts that Paul and Angeline had seen. It brought a sense of relief to know they were not alone on planet Earth. The survivors were attempting to put their lives back together and restore order to their shattered worlds.

"I want to see if I can find anyone at the local R.C.M.P. who can go back to retrieve Tom's body and bring those other two criminals in as well," Paul commented as they headed toward the town center.

"Do you think O'Kelly is still alive?" Angeline asked apprehensively.

"I don't think I killed him."

"He deserved to be killed," she responded

He spotted an opened convenience store that had a long line of weary customers. Pulling over, he hoped to buy coffee, but discovered there were no hot beverages. The shop was doing a heavy trade in anything cold and edible as the electricity had not yet been restored.

After he had purchased buns and soda, he asked the manager for directions to the local police station. The shop assistant told him not to expect too much assistance as the police already had their hands full.

He returned to the vehicle to wait for Angeline who had gone to find the washroom. She finally returned, complaining that there was no running water.

They left and followed the directions given by the shop assistant to the police station. Several people stood outside the entrance when they arrived. Paul and Angeline pushed their way past an angry looking man who glared at them and said, "It's no use trying to get any help here!"

"Why?" Paul asked.

"There's only one person on duty and she's inundated with calls. Everyone's using public phones and the radio's blaring. I don't think she can cope."

Paul took Angeline by the hand and pushed through the door. There were more people inside, some sitting, others standing; everyone talking at the same time. The duty officer sat with the phone in one hand and the radio receiver in the other.

She looked up as Paul and Angeline approached the counter. "Just about everyone in town is trying to get through to us. I'll be with you in a moment."

She was a young woman in her twenties and appeared to be lacking in experience. Paul waited for a minute while she ended a conversation on the radio. When she ignored him and returned to the telephone again he became a little impatient.

"Can you help me—I'm in a hurry."

She looked up at him and scowled. He tried again.

"I want to report a murder."

"Please, be patient."

"I have to get down to Victoria."

She ignored him and continued with the telephone conversation. He looked at Angeline and shook his head. After another minute of intense conversation the officer replaced the receiver and looked enquiringly at Paul. "What did you say about a murder?"

He told her briefly about the shooting of Tom Wilson.

"We don't have the manpower to cope with this at the moment. Leave it with me and I will get someone to attend to it."

The phone rang again and the radio crackled to life, almost simultaneously.

"You'll need to write this all down!" Paul responded in exasperation.

She glared at him and placed her hand over the receiver. "Can't you see there's pandemonium in here? I can't do everything immediately! We have so much to deal with right now that I can't see anyone going out there for a couple of days. You'll just have to exercise some patience!"

Paul wanted to vent his frustration but decided it wouldn't help. "But what am I supposed to do?"

The officer shrugged and then continued with the phone conversation.

Paul could see he was wasting his time. He turned and they walked away, leaving the flustered officer to do battle with the demands of the telephone and radio.

"I need to find an open gas station," said Paul as they walked down the street to the Jeep. "I think I have half a tank, which should be enough to get us to Victoria. The downside is we don't know what other detours we might have to make to get there."

Paul drove around several of the streets looking for a gas station but unfortunately there was no electricity available so none of the gas stations were open for business. Finally, needing a quick bathroom break, he pulled in at a hotel and they were fortunate to find the facilities open with an intact water supply.

∞

Twelve

Convenient Transport.
Tuesday, 7:35 a.m. 26th September.

O'Kelly and Banville, aided by a flashlight from the Land Cruiser, had walked for nine hours before they reached the landslide which temporarily stopped Paul and Angeline. Despite the long trek, O'Kelly had recovered his strength and was determined to press on.

They continued on their journey, hoping to find some sign of life, or an abandoned vehicle that might provide transport. An hour later they came across exactly what they had hoped to find. A car parked off the road next to a stream—an older, green Ford Fusion.

The occupants were nowhere in sight and had perhaps walked down to the stream to check it out before the earthquake had taken place. The doors were locked and O'Kelly did not hesitate to search for a suitable rock with which to break the glass window.

With the door promptly opened, Banville took a few minutes to hotwire the ignition and they were on their way, giving hearty thanks to the hapless stranger who had so conveniently provided transport. Another convenient provision was the nearly full gas tank.

A further hour of driving brought O'Kelly and Banville to Port Alberni midmorning. Both were tired and hungry so O'Kelly drove around looking for an open shop. Eventually they spotted cars parked in the Tim Horton parking area, further up the main street. They parked their vehicle and entered the building to find the attendants had fired up two gas stoves for making fresh pots of coffee.

Banville bought two take-out coffees and they walked back to the vehicle, savoring the aroma and warmth the beverages brought to their weary bodies.

They climbed back into the vehicle and drove up the main street until they reached the next intersection. There were no traffic lights working and everyone on the road treated intersections as four-way stops. While they were waiting for a truck that arrived seconds before to cross, Banville made an excited exclamation, "Shit! Isn't that their Jeep over there?"

He pointed to a white vehicle parked in a hotel's parking area along the adjacent side street.

O'Kelly stared for a brief moment. "It looks like theirs—we'll take a quick look. Good spotting, Andre."

He turned right at the corner and pulled into the hotel grounds, parking close to the front entrance.

"Now we can even the score," said O'Kelly excitedly.

"The only problem is that he has your gun," said Banville.

"We'll just have to take them by surprise and relieve him of it. My guess is they are making a pit-stop in the hotel here—let's see if we can get the drop on them; the last people they should expect to see would be us," answered O'Kelly with conviction.

The two men crept around to the hotel's front entrance and carefully checked the foyer. There was nobody there so they walked down the hallway to the washroom signs and stopped outside the entrance to the "ladies."

O'Kelly listened intently and said, "I can hear the sounds of running water. It might be the woman—we'll grab her when she comes out."

Banville produced a clasp knife from his pocket and opened the blade, brandishing it with enthusiasm. "At least we have something we can use," he said eagerly—"that prick, Brinkworth, will think twice about using the gun if we threaten to slit his girlfriend's throat."

O'Kelly nodded and waited just beyond the entrance. The "gents" washroom was adjacent and they could hear the noise of a toilet being flushed. Banville nodded, and suspecting it might be Paul Brinkworth, moved into a position where he could surprise the seismologist when he egressed. They did not have long to wait.

A few moments later Angeline came out and was taken from behind by O'Kelly who spoke softly but deliberately. "Keep quiet and I won't hurt you."

Angeline, paralyzed with fear, did not make a sound as O'Kelly clamped his hand over her mouth. Banville quickly passed the knife to the Irishman and returned to his position outside the "gents" to wait for Paul Brinkworth.

They waited a short while before Paul made his exit from the washroom. Banville stood silently beyond the exit and did nothing, waiting to see Paul's reaction to O'Kelly, who held Angeline with his one arm tightly around her waist and the knife at her throat.

Paul was startled into immobility when he saw them. O'Kelly sneered at him and said, "Well, Brinkworth—we meet under different circumstances, yet again."

Paul quickly found his voice. "Don't hurt her, O'Kelly. Why the fuck can't you leave us alone?"

O'Kelly was quick to answer, "We can't let you get away with what you've found out, Brinkworth. Besides, I have a score to settle with you."

"Then settle that score with me and leave her out of it—we're not interested in your little caper back in the rainforest. We just want to get to our families."

Banville laughed. "You think we're that stupid, motherfucker? Where's the gun?"

Paul glared at him but said nothing further.

O'Kelly smiled. "He must have left it in the vehicle. Give us the keys Brinkworth."

Once again, Paul felt he had to acquiesce to the request for fear that they might hurt Angeline. He threw the keys to Banville who immediately left to search Paul's Jeep. It took a few minutes for him to find the weapon which Paul had wrapped in a cloth and hidden in the spare-wheel well.

There was still no receptionist at the desk when he got back from searching the Jeep so O'Kelly, still holding Angeline tightly said, "Look behind the counter and get us a key to an empty room. We'll stop here for a while and I'll try to get ahold of Rushmore."

*

The first thing O'Kelly had done after they marched Paul and Angeline to an empty room was to tie Angeline's hands behind her back with a lamp's electrical cord. The end of the cord was tied to her feet so she couldn't move. She was then unceremoniously dumped on the bathroom floor and before closing the door O'Kelly growled, "Stay in there and don't move. If you do, we'll shoot your boyfriend."

Then they set about getting even with Paul. Paul prepared to protect himself when O'Kelly approached with obvious intent of giving him a beating. There was not too much he could do with Banville holding the gun on him and after trying to defend himself with raised arms he took a shot on the jaw from the Irishman that stunned him momentarily. After that he lost consciousness.

O'Kelly took out his anger on the seismologist's inert body, kicking him in the ribs and head with free abandon until he ran out of strength. Finally, he sat on the bed and listened to the sobbing that came from Angeline in the bathroom.

"Feel better, Sean?" asked Banville, checking to see if Paul was still alive—he was.

O'Kelly's eyes were glazed with fulfilment. Things could not be better.

He sat, without moving until his breath evened out and then reached for the phone. As he expected, no dial tone.

"Keep an eye on these two turds and if Brinkworth wakes up before I get back don't allow him in with his girlfriend, or her out here with him. Understood?"

Banville grinned. "Whatever you say, Sean."

O'Kelly left the room and headed down to the foyer. It was not that far to the payphones at the local post office. Passing the reception desk he went outside and was about to get into the Jeep when he

176

realized that Banville had the keys. Feeling sore and tired he decided to use the car they had stolen—the two ignition wires had been separated while not in use and it took a simple action to twist them together to start the car.

The Irishman arrived outside the post office to find all booths, bar one, were in use. He called Rushmore's home number but it went to voicemail so he decided to see if Hilda was at home. After a few rings, O'Kelly was gratified to hear her voice but she on the other hand, was not overjoyed to hear the bad news.

"You had better take care of this, Sean! I don't want to be the one to tell Rushmore the operation's been blown. Everything we've built over the past five years is in jeopardy because of your incompetence."

"Don't talk to me about incompetence! You weren't there to see what happened, so just keep your fucking mouth shut."

Hilda stemmed the ilk she felt on the rise. "It just so happens that Rushmore's in Nanaimo at the moment. He came up yesterday morning to our outlet store at the mall and couldn't get back to Victoria because of the earthquake so he booked into the Coast Bastion for the night. He is presently with Gus at the shop."

"I need to speak with him urgently. I'm on a payphone here at the PO in Alberni," said O'Kelly with a more conciliatory tone of voice.

Hilda thought for a moment before answering. "I will drive down there and let him know what's going on. Give me the payphone's number."

O'Kelly gave it to her and hung up. There was nothing more to do except wait for Rushmore to call. At least he had some good news—Rushmore could decide what to do with Brinkworth and his girlfriend. He sat on a bench near the booth and lit a cigarette.

After fifteen minutes Rushmore called the booth and O'Kelly jumped up at the sudden sound of the phone ringing. He picked up the receiver.

"What the fuck's going on, Sean!"

The Irishman explained what had taken place since the earthquake; everything except the killing of Tom Wilson. He knew that Rushmore did not like his employees to take things into their own hands—if anything regarding the matter was exposed he would claim self-defense, which in his mind, it was. Rushmore was the kind that jumped to conclusions and it was best to keep things as simple as possible.

"Be glad you came across this Brinkworth shithead again," growled Rushmore unimpressed. "We have a lot riding on that operation, Sean. Make sure you do things exactly as I tell you. Bring them here to Hilda's place—I have an idea."

O'Kelly reassured Rushmore he would not allow anything to go wrong and was about to hang up the receiver when the boss added one more thing. "Oh, and if you need to get ahold of me again for any reason, text me. The cell service is overwhelmed but texting seems to get through easier."

O'Kelly left the post office feeling better now that any further decisions regarding his prisoners would be taken by Rushmore. He twirled the ignition wires together and headed back to the hotel.

*

Banville kept a watchful eye on Paul Brinkworth who lay quietly on the floor next to the queen-size bed. Brinkworth appeared be out for the count. A wound had opened on the back of his head and blood trickled down onto his shirt collar. Both eyebrows and one cheek had started to swell and his nose had been bleeding; *a sorry sight* thought Banville .

Angeline had stopped sobbing and was repeatedly crying out Paul's name. She sensed someone was still in the room besides Paul and she pleaded to be let out.

Banville was annoyed at first but thought it might be time to have some fun with the girl. Brinkworth was certainly not going to offer any resistance in his present state and besides, he thought, I can keep an eye on the sucker while enjoying myself! He smirked as he reminded himself of O'Kelly's departing words; not to allow the two prisoners to be together.

Banville had always been a rebellious person who never liked taking orders, even from his early childhood. Who was O'Kelly to deny him pleasure anyway? And it wasn't as if he was going to allow the two to be together—one was unconscious and the other defenseless.

He approached the bathroom, revolver in hand, with one thing on his mind.

On opening the door he looked down at the woman still lying where O'Kelly had dumped her. Despite Angeline's disheveled appearance, he admired her obvious beauty. He rolled her onto her back, and realized to carry out his intentions he had to untie her feet.

After maneuvering Angeline's trussed-up body into the small bedroom, Banville lifted her onto the second queen bed and wasted no time untying the electrical cord from her hands and feet. "Just so you know," he said with a grin and started to undo his belt buckle—"I have no problem hitting a woman. I'd hate to mess-up your pretty fa..."

Angeline's right foot moved with surprising speed, catching Banville in the groin with all the force she could muster.

She instinctively rolled over, falling off the bed and onto her knees. At that moment Paul who had just begun to regained his consciousness, heard the commotion followed by a loud exclamation from Banville. The big man slumped backward grabbing his crotch with both hands.

The heavy lampstand with broken-off electric cord, was lying on the floor in line with Paul's eyesight—instinctively he knew what had happened and what he needed to do. It took an immense effort of willpower to overcome the weak feeling in is body and react to the situation. Snatching up the lamp he raised himself onto his knees; a rush of dizziness persisted as he started to stand on shaky legs. Banville was bending toward him, doubled over as a result of Angeline's vicious but well-aimed kick. Paul raised the lamp as high as he could and then smashed it down on their captor's head.

Banville went out like a light. He lay deathly still on the floor while blood started to ooze its way down his neck and onto the carpet.

*

On O'Kelly's return to the hotel he sensed immediately something was wrong. Brinkworth's

Jeep was gone. He hurriedly parked the car and in a blind panic shot through the entrance into the foyer, drawing a glance from the now present receptionist.

"Can I help you, sir?" she shouted as he tore past.

O'Kelly didn't answer and continued on his headlong flight, taking the stairs three at a time and breathing hard. He found the door to the room open, kindling his worst fears—the prisoners had escaped.

Andre lay on the floor, his comatose form saying it all. *I knew I should never have left the fucker alone with Brinkworth!*

O'Kelly tried to revive Banville but got no reaction. He felt for a pulse and detected a very feint sign of life—then taking Banville's head in both hands he braced himself and said, "Sleep peacefully, Andre."

*

There was nothing else to be done in the room so O'Kelly rushed downstairs to the reception counter.

"Did you see two people leave the hotel within the last ten minutes or so?" he shouted at the receptionist, a woman he judged to be in her early thirties.

"Yes, a man and woman just left. They didn't stop when I asked them if they were hotel patrons—just hurried on out."

O'Kelly left the receptionist standing behind the desk, her mouth open. When he had twirled the ignition wires and started the engine he quickly pulled out his cell phone to text Rushmore. He was angry at Banville's bungling and scared of having to tell Rushmore the truth, but it had to be done. Rushmore would hunt him down if he left things as they were; besides, there might be a chance his boss could do something to apprehend Brinkworth and the woman.

The answer came quicker than he thought it would. The jingle of the phone sounded as he was speeding over the summit of the Arrowsmith Mountain pass, east of Port Alberni and heading toward the main island freeway.

The text from Rushmore was to the point:

Will apprehend vehicle at on-ramp to m-freeway, before QC—follow up behind—leaving now.

O'Kelly held the phone on top of the steering wheel and punched away at the keyboard: *Will explain later.*

He drove furiously, hoping to catch sight of Brinkworth's Jeep.

∞

Thirteen

A Familiar Enemy.
Tuesday, 11:30 a.m. 26th September.

Paul and Angeline, having left the hotel, made for the highway that led to Nanaimo and then onto Victoria. Angeline wouldn't answer any of Paul's probing questions regarding her wellbeing. She sat in silent contemplation wiping at Paul's bloodied face and neck with a wet hotel washcloth .

There were several minor landslides that encroached onto the road and slowed their progress but not enough to cause any real concern. Very few vehicles were on the road, creating the perception that circumstances on the ravaged island were still far from normal. That fact caused Paul to be suspicious of the green vehicle following them. It had appeared suddenly and was maintaining a consistent distance behind them.

Angeline saw his continuous glances at the rear view-mirror and turned to stare at the following vehicle.

"Is something wrong?" she inquired, her voice shaking slightly.

Paul licked his swollen lip. "The thought occurred to me that we have been virtually the only ones on the road since we left Tofino yesterday. Now I've noticed that vehicle behind us."

Angeline turned again to look at the vehicle. Paul kept shooting glances into the side-mirror.

"It hasn't gained or lost any following distance since we left Alberni."

"You're not thinking what I'm thinking are you?" Angeline queried tentatively.

"O'Kelly? I doubt it."

Angeline twisted in her seat but the vehicle was too far behind for her to see the occupants. "Do you think O'Kelly's helper survived? He looked very dead when we left the room."

"I didn't stop to check him—his name's Andre. I heard O'Kelly talking to him before they attacked me."

Paul increased speed slightly before throwing another glance at the mirror. The vehicle behind quickly matched the speed of the Jeep.

They passed through Cathedral Grove, its towering trees dwarfing the Jeep as though it was a toy. Several trees had fallen during the earthquake but none directly across the road. One behemoth had fallen at an angle, but was caught in the trees, suspended like a bridge over the paving. The Jeep easily passed underneath without slowing.

The freeway began to twist and turn, obscuring the view of the vehicle behind them. Paul immediately accelerated and when the green car came into view again it had lost considerable ground on them.

"We'll see if they catch up to us again," ventured Paul.

Angeline turned again in her seat and glanced nervously through the back window. "What will we do if it is O'Kelly?"

"I would be really surprised if it is. I won't let them get too close," Paul replied.

They drove for several miles before the vehicle behind caught up its following distance which it maintained until they passed the turnoff to Coombs. The driver of the green car, accelerated.

Angeline stared out the rear window and froze as she recognized the familiar face behind the wheel. It was O'Kelly. His facial expression showed no emotion.

They were approaching the interchange outside the small town of Qualicum Beach. Paul saw that the bridge overpass had collapsed but the Nanaimo onramp appeared to be intact. On approaching, red emergency markers across the on-ramp entrance caught his eye. The reason suddenly became frighteningly evident.

A gasoline tanker-trailer had flipped onto its side in the center of the onramp. There appeared to be no room for the Jeep to pass safely at their speed—a disaster in the making.

Paul's mind took in the scene, his eyes raking the area ahead to secure some way out of the hopeless situation that confronted them.

Within a second, he'd make a decision to either hit the gasoline tanker-trailer, or swerve and collide with the freeway's road barrier.

Their speed was too great to swing across without capsizing, so there was really no alternative and he prepared for impact. Then his eye picked up a gap between the rear of the trailer and the left-hand metal barrier.

The eight-foot gap provided precious little space to force the speeding vehicle through. If he misjudged by six inches and hit the back of the trailer they were as good as dead.

He put the Jeep into a controlled slide, aiming the front fender at the back-end of the trailer's fuel compartment. As the Jeep was traversing the narrow space its right, front fender scraped against the back of the trailer, causing a shower of sparks to fly in all directions.

Fearing the sudden ignition of leaking gasoline Paul stamped on the accelerator. The Jeep seemed to linger for a brief second between trailer and barrier before the rear wheels bit into the soft soil on the road's edge, pushing them through the gap. They teetered on the road's shoulder with the right side of the Jeep lifting into the air while Paul desperately fought with the steering. The grounded wheels slipped over the verge into looser soil, causing the back of the Jeep to slew dangerously toward the left before he managed to gain a measure of control. In what seemed to take an eternity the vehicle righted itself.

The sudden jolt of exploding fuel propelled them forward. The gasoline in the second of the two compartments ignited, demolishing the trailer and searing the backend of the Jeep as it passed through the narrow opening. Paul felt the vehicle pull heavily to the right side and a thought instantly struck him: *flat front tire.*

A heavy vibration started on the passenger side of the Jeep and he realized they would have to pull over or risk shredding the tire completely. He aimed for the onramp's right shoulder and started bringing the vehicle to a stop.

As they slowed down, a black van partly obscured by some low bushes, pulled onto the road and stopped in the middle of the onramp, right in front of them. Paul had no option but to stamp hard on the brake pedal and bring the Jeep to a dead-stop. Feeling a little bewildered, he slowly unclipped the safety belt and looked across at Angeline. "Are you okay?"

She sat motionless, staring ahead at the van. The fear in her voice was palpable as she tried to muster a little composure. "What happened to O'Kelly? Why is this vehicle blocking our way?"

Paul looked over his shoulder but could not see anything but thick, black smoke. "I don't think O'Kelly made it through that gap—I would be surprised if he did. Stay here."

He opened the driver's door and stepped onto the road, walking around to the right side front of the Jeep to check the tire—he was not surprised see it was completely flat. While he contemplated getting out the jack from the spare-wheel well, a noise from the van drew his attention.

Two men, one from each side of the van, came walking toward the Jeep. One was short and stocky, the other tall and slender. Paul did not recognize either of the men but then a woman appeared beside the taller of the two and his blood suddenly ran cold. He recognized her immediately. It was the woman who had been with O'Kelly in the rainforest on their first encounter.

Paul stood his ground. Just when he thought they had escaped, more trouble appeared to be looming for them. Angeline unclipped her seatbelt and opened the passenger side door, stepping down onto the roadway beside Paul. She took his hand in hers as the two groups faced off.

The tall, slender man looked questioningly at Hilda who nodded. Then he turned toward Paul again and said, "I understand you've been meddling in my affairs."

Seeing Hilda, Paul quickly put things together. "How so?"

Rushmore's eyes were like steel. "You have witnessed our little operation at the rainforest and we need to talk. I insist that you accompany us to Nanaimo."

"There's nothing to talk about—we're not going anywhere with you," said Paul gruffly.

The tall man produced a gun that had been hidden from view, behind his back. He spoke to the short, stocky man. "Tie their hands, Gus."

Gus walked around behind the couple and pulled out several zip-ties from his pocket, plus a roll of duct tape. Paul was not going to be hijacked so easily and whipped around, with his fists raised, to face Gus. The tall man stepped quickly to Angeline's side and snatched her arm, placing the revolver against her temple. "Stand down, Brinkworth—unless you want me to harm your girlfriend."

Paul felt overwhelmed. His body was still stiff and sore from the beating O'Kelly had handed out. Thinking better of the situation he decided to wait for a more compliant opportunity. Angeline had switched off into a world of her own emotional trauma and offered no resistance to her captors. Her nightmare was starting over again.

Rushmore walked quickly to the edge of the collapsed overpass and peered at the scene at the bottom of the onramp. The sight that greeted his eyes made him flinch. The trailer had exploded in a blaze of ignited gasoline and the wreck of a green car lay beyond the road barrier, burning fiercely. A man in a blue shirt was bending over a horribly burned body just beyond the barrier. Rushmore knew it had to be O'Kelly lying there; a thin smile adorned his lips. "Well, that takes care of him."

He walked back to the vehicle where the others were waiting at the van's open, sliding door. The short, stocky man, Gus, looked enquiringly at Rushmore, but Rushmore simply said, "O'Kelly's no longer with us." He eyed the two prisoners on the metal cargo floor and handed Hilda the gun. "Hilda, look after them while Gus and I change the Jeep's wheel."

Hilda Rogers sat in the front passenger seat of the van, with the revolver held tightly in her hand. The captives appeared strangely subdued. She had expected a little more fire from them but they sat quietly amongst the boxes of Hurricane Charley both seemingly resigned to their fate. She had no idea what Rushmore had planned for them. She looked at Angeline who seemed to be totally zoned out of the present situation and felt sorry for her. Suddenly Angeline swung her head and looked Hilda in the eye—a primal message conveying the

191

struggle of the disadvantaged woman, abused by the opposite sex, passed between them and Hilda shuddered, turning away to look out the side window.

The product of a rough, lower class neighborhood in Toronto, Ontario where she learned to fend for herself at an early age, Hilda had struggled against the oppression of certain men. She was an attractive brunette with a firm, shapely body and all the curves in the right places. Her relationships with men, in general, had not been positive.

Life had been hard in the early years, exacerbated by the loss of her mother. Her mental health had suffered when the stepfather she hated, abused her from the day her mother died, until her sixteenth year.

Deciding life could not get any worse Hilda had run away from home, seeking asylum with an aunt of whom she knew little. That stay was brief. The aunt, divorced and uneducated, had turned to prostitution in an effort to support them.

It was not long before she introduced Hilda back into the world of abuse. This unfortunate lifestyle ended abruptly one night when a client tried to strangle her in a drunken frenzy.

She barely escaped with her life. Fortunately the man's strength failed due to an overdose of whiskey and she escaped through the bedroom window.

The experience hardened her even further against men and she became determined to be self-supporting. However, opportunities for honest occupations providing good incomes, for those who were not well educated, had not presented themselves.

At the age of nineteen she met a member of the syndicate who used a bathroom-product organization of corporate shops for selling hard drugs. It did not take her long to decide that selling drugs was far more lucrative than selling her body at night and waiting on tables during the day.

The only executive member she had ever met was Barry Rushmore. Although condescending, he had never tried to take advantage of her. She had been attracted to him at first until she got to know him. One night several years back he had needed to stay over in Nanaimo and she had offered her place. Knowing he was a bit of a womanizer it did not seem harmful to share her bed with him. She soon found out, however, that Rushmore's idea of sex wasn't what she was looking for. From that night on she'd been scared of him and tried to keep their relationship as professional as possible.

Her flashback was rudely interrupted when Rushmore appeared at the driver's door and climbed into the vehicle.

"Gus will drive the Jeep back to Nanaimo," he said looking across at her. "Keep your eye on those two in the back. We're going back to the shop."

Hilda glanced nervously toward the back of the van. "What are you going to do with them, Barry?"

Rushmore simply smiled and said, "I have a plan. Don't you worry about a thing."

∞

Fourteen

Imprisonment.
Tuesday, 2:30 p.m. 26th September.

Paul was bundled out of the van and into the back entrance of a shop at the Wooldgrove shopping center. A storeroom packed with different sorts of upmarket bathroom products awaited him. Gus removed the duct tape from his mouth as Rushmore entered.

Paul felt a sudden panic rising when Angelline was not brought in with him.

He turned to face Rushmore and asked with a shaky voice, "Where's the woman? Why is she not with me?"

Rushmore smiled and answered, "I have plans for her, Brinkworth, but you're just a liability."

"Go to Fodding hell!" shouted Paul with venom. "Do what you want with me but let the woman go."

"I'm afraid that is out of the question," said Rushmore and with a nod at Gus, calmly walked out of the storeroom.

Paul, now terrified at what they might do to Angelline shouted, "What do you mean, out of the question? Come back here and talk to me you shithead."

Gus pushed Paul down into a sitting position and sealed Paul's mouth with the duct tape again. He then left, locking the door behind him.

Hilda had waited in the van while Rushmore dealt with Brinkworth. She had a feeling of apprehension as to why the woman had been left with her but she tried to play it down. After ten minutes Rushmore returned and they left for Hilda's house. Gus, the manager of the outlet shop, had sent the shop's other server home and would remain there by himself until Rushmore returned.

Hilda had worked on and off in the shop at various times. It had fitted in well with her other duties at the lab in the rainforest but she was glad that Gus had offered to stay. She wanted to get back home.

*

Rushmore and Hilda sat around the dining room table, drinking Merlot. They had forced Angeline to take a sedative due to her continuous sobbing, which had begun the moment Paul had been taken from the van, at the store. Her hands and feet were tightly secured by zip ties—she appeared to have mercifully fallen asleep on the bed in the spare room.

Hilda felt badly for Angeline. It was, as had been her experience, the greatest weakness of all men. They just couldn't resist a good-looking woman and she unconsciously placed herself in this same category. She had been fortunate to have escaped Rushmore's clutches but had often caught him admiring her figure whenever they met, which was usually at the shop. Her thinking was that Rushmore had felt slighted after that one occasion when, after too many drinks, they had both wound up in bed and he tried some kinky bondage sex. She had immediately refused and left his hotel room. They had never mentioned it again and since that time he had behaved himself, however, she knew he was always watching her.

Rushmore broke the uneasy silence. "I'm not going back to the hotel—I'll be staying here tonight."

Hilda looked at him suspiciously, waiting for a further explanation.

After a hesitation, seeing the look on Hilda's face, he added, "I only booked the one night and I believe the hotel is full. I'm going to use one of the beds in your spare room—if you don't mind."

"Suite yourself," said Hilda as casually as she could, her suspicions as to Rushmore's real intentions, on the rise.

"Gus and I will take care of Brinkworth and the woman in the early hours of the morning—a good time when no one else is around."

She became alarmed at the insidious intent of his words. He could mean only one thing. In all her years of working with Rushmore she realized she really knew very little about him. At no time during that tenure had she known anyone to have been murdered but now she suspected that this might not be the case. The thought crossed her mind; *could Rushmore be that cold-blooded?*

Hilda shuddered and looked into her glass, swirling the wine around in contemplation. "And the girl?" she asked guardedly.

"I won't bother her," he said with a thin smile.

Hilda detected his exact intentions and looked away, suddenly hating Rushmore for his callous attitude.

I wonder if he won't do this to me too, one day—she thought with alarm. It seemed an impulsive act on her behalf but in that moment she made her decision.

Later that evening after they had eaten dinner Rushmore said, "I'm going to turn in. Gus and I have a busy morning ahead of us."

"What time are you going to leave?" she asked.

"At four-thirty, before the sun comes up. Gus will be here to take Brinkworth's Jeep and I'll drive the van."

"Where will you take them?" asked Hilda, trying not to allow panic to show in her voice.

"To the old deserted mill next to HARMAC—near the ferry terminal at Duke Point. We should be back by six-thirty or so, but in case we aren't, I need you to open the shop at the usual time," Rushmore concluded as he headed for the spare room.

"Okay—whatever you say, Barry." Hilda's heart was in her throat. The full impact of being an accessory to murder suddenly hit her. She ran through the house to the privacy of the bedroom and slammed the door. The conflicting emotions between the need to protect her livelihood and the fear of being involved in Rushmore's evil plan had finally come to a head—she plunged into the en-suite bathroom and lost her dinner.

A few minutes later Hilda sat down on the side of the bathtub. It was time to get her act together and think more constructively about her plight. She glanced at her bedside clock: 8:00 p.m.

Rushmore took a quick shower in the second bathroom next to the spare room. His senses were heightened by the day's excitement and he looked forward to ending it with the fulfillment of a thought that had captivated his mind since he had first laid eyes on Angeline, earlier that day.

He didn't even bother to pull on his clothes after the shower but exited naked, carrying his small overnight suitcase in one hand, into the spare room. There were two single beds, opposite each other and on one of them lay Angeline, sleeping quietly and peacefully under the influence of the pill they had given her earlier.

Rushmore delved into his overnight case and pulled out a knife with which he cut the zip-ties that tied Angeline's hands and ankles together—he had been waiting several hours for this moment.

*

The storeroom was not very large. Boxes of bathroom products were stacked everywhere and Paul, with his hands and ankles tied, had difficulty in finding comfortable position on the floor. Not that comfort was uppermost on his mind, on the contrary. He worried about Angeline but in his present plight there was nothing he could do. He had tried everything to break the cable ties that bound him. There was nothing in the room that he could see, to sever them so he resigned himself to his present fate. He was sure of one thing: they would be back to finalize any plan they had for him and Angeline.

The tall, slender man who appeared to be the boss had a womanizer appearance about him and Paul feared for Angeline's wellbeing. She had already suffered the near violation of her body once that day—would it happen again? He did not want to think along those lines, so instead he thought about the time he and Angeline had spent together—the soft feel of her silky, smooth skin against his own and the warmth of her breath on his neck when he held her close. He would do anything to help her escape the mess they were both in.

Exhausted from the day's events he finally fell asleep in a sitting position with his back leaning against a wall.

**

Tuesday, 4:40 p.m. 26th September.

The Nanaimo General Hospital received a steady stream of injured people from the surrounding area in the wake of the earthquake.

Friends and relatives were responsible for bringing in many of the victims. One such admission was the man brought in by Ryan Kaufman, the driver of the overturned tanker-trailer near Qualicum Beach.

The victim was barely recognizable as a human being. His condition was so serious the local clinics of Qualicum and Parksville could not deal with him. His condition had been complicated by severe burns sustained when his vehicle collided with the rear of the over-turned tanker-trailer.

Kaufman had been able to revive the man sufficiently to save his life and get him to the hospital. Technically he was a John Doe with no way of establishing his identity until he regained consciousness.

Kaufman offered no explanation on behalf of the victim and finally left to make his way back to Port Alberni, where he lived.

The injured man underwent immediate surgery and was then wheeled through to a recovery room. The nurse on duty was told to get his particulars when he was conscious enough to talk. They were extremely short staffed and under pressure, which meant patients were not receiving adequate care.

The man regained consciousness two days later and gave the nurse a false name and address. He said there were no other family members who could help him.

The duty nurse in charge of the ward was not able to confirm his identity as the earthquake had damaged the internet nodes in the area. It would be many days before any of the ensuing administration would be straightened out.

**

Tuesday, 8:15 p.m. 26th September.

Hilda was trying to pluck up courage to leave her room. She heard Rushmore go into the spare room after his shower and was under no illusions as to what he was up to. The spare room door closed and she knew she had to take her chances. An idea had begun to form in her mind requiring only about five minutes to expedite but she needed go outside to Brinkworth's Jeep, parked in the driveway—time was of the essence if she was to give the two prisoners a fighting chance.

She crept through the living room to the kitchen door and stepped onto the driveway that led to the garage that housed the Jeep. Her own car had been parked in the street as Rushmore wasn't taking any chances of the Jeep being recognized.

It was highly unlikely that would happen as everyone was still getting their lives together after the quake. Electricity was still a problem and only a few residential areas had power. The streets were dark and no traffic lights were working anywhere in the city. Having to open the shop seemed unnecessary to her as there were few people about. Maybe Rushmore was afraid of looters. There appeared to be only one service station open in the whole of the city, perhaps the only one still to have power. Walmart had managed to stay open and

203

there were long lines as people, who had not been prepared for the disaster, waited patiently to get the last remaining items left on the shelves.

The garage at the back was open and Hilda crept up to the backdoor of the Jeep. It was not locked and she quickly found what she was looking for. Paul had left his backpack lying on the floor behind the backseat and it took her half a minute to find what she had hoped would be in it—his cell phone.

Fortunately it still had a charge. Then she panicked when she realized she did not have the password, something she had not thought of. There was only one thing to do. She guessed Rushmore would be busy for hours so it was worth taking the chance. Her car keys lay on the kitchen table where she had left them.

The mall was almost deserted, save Walmart. She parked at the rear entrance to the shop and opened the backdoor with her key. The storeroom was never usually locked so Gus was the only one who had its key.

Quietly she walked up to the storeroom door and listened. All was quiet.

"Mr. Brinworth!" she called out hoping he was still there; that Gus hadn't moved him.

She heard a rustling sound, a box of product fell to the floor and a gruff voice answered her.

"Who's there?"

"I'm going to try to help you—not to escape, but to make contact with someone who could perhaps come to your aid," answered Hilda.

"If you want to help me, why don't you just unlock the door," said Paul.

"I can't do that. If Rushmore finds out he'll kill me," she answered back.

"Rushmore. Is that the prick running the show?" asked Paul feeling a surge of revulsion at the thought of the man.

"You ask too many questions," returned Hilda angrily. "If you want me to help you then give me the password to your phone."

Paul was silent for a moment and then deciding there was nothing to lose, he said, "Earthquake, with a capital E."

"Is there anyone whom you think would be able to help you?" she asked.

Paul gave it some thought. This was a huge responsibility and he struggled to think of someone, who under the circumstances, would have the means and be free.

Finally he made a decision, "My wife, Megan. You'll find her number under 'Meg' in my contacts."

"I hope she'll be able to do something. Rushmore intends to kill you and the woman tomorrow morning."

Paul felt a cold sweat break out on his brow when he heard the words. "Where is my friend?" he asked, hoping to hear some news of Angeline.

Hilda told a half lie, "She's asleep—don't worry about her. I am going to call your wife and I hope she doesn't think it a prank but that's why I need to use your phone. I'll give her as much information as I think necessary and it'll be up to her."

Hilda left the building and drove quickly back to her house. On arrival she crept inside and heard moans coming from the spare room. Once in her bedroom she locked the door and sat on the bed with Brinworth's phone. The fact that Megan Brinkworth would recognize the number from which the call would come increased the chance of her not taking it as someone trying to play a sick joke.

She found the number and tapped the phone icon.

∞

Fifteen

Hilda's Fateful Text.
Tuesday, 8:45 p.m. 26th September.

Amy sat on the bed in her room and stared blankly at the wall for a few seconds. She stifled the temptation to cry and forced herself to bring perspective to everything the text message on her mother's phone told her.

Lillian, who had decided to stay at her son's home until the return of one of the parents, came into the bedroom and hesitantly touched Amy's shoulder. They looked at each other for a moment and then Lillian asked, "Was that your father, dear?"

Amy took a few seconds to find her voice.

"No. It was some person trying to contact Mom but, of course, I have the phone. Whoever it was said that Daddy and a friend need help urgently—that I need to find someone who would be prepared to go to Nanaimo to save them."

"Why didn't this person go to the Nanaimo police, dear—can you ask?" questioned Lillian, concerned for her son's safety.

Amy nodded and did the return text.

Ten seconds later the reply came back.

"The Nanaimo police are too busy because their hands are full with the aftermath of the quake. It needs for someone to do something immediately. Whoever we find to help us needs to be at the old deserted mill next to HARMAC, near Duke Point before five tomorrow morning."

"And what is supposed to happen there?" asked Lillian, now extremely anxious.

"Because Daddy's life is in danger and that some very bad men are going to kill him."

Lillian ran to the house phone and dialed 911. The line was busy. In a panic she grabbed the phone book and looked on the front page for the number of the local police. After what seemed like an eternity a woman answered. Lillian made a harrowing attempt to tell the woman about the text she had just received but after several questions it was clear that the officer thought it was a prank. Eventually she cut Lillian off and told her to call the Nanaimo police.

Lillian stood with the phone in her hand and cried tears of frustration. Suddenly Amy had an idea.

"Do you have Dan's number, Gran? I'm sure he'll help us...we must try everything to help Dad."

"Do I have his number? Oh yes—I remember, he gave me his card. It's in my handbag."

Dan answered the call straight away and after asking for directions to the Brinkworth home he assured Amy he would be there within half an hour.

"Where is your brother, dear?" Lillian asked, perplexed that she had not seen Jason for a while.

"He's next door with his friend, Peter. Do you want me to call him?" answered Amy

"No, dear. It's probably just as well he know nothing about this."

True to his word Dan arrived at the house thirty minutes later. Sultan, perched in the back of the truck, barked excitedly. He ruffled the shepherd's ears and walked quickly to the front door, giving three sharp raps.

Amy let him in and they stood in the living room while she related all the news regarding the strange text. She showed Dan the details on Meg's phone and the South African studied them, word for word.

Finally, after considering the details, he said, "I don't think we should try to get the police involved — they're far too busy."

"Will you help us?" pleaded Amy tearfully.

"Sure. But I need to clear it with my boss."

Dan called Ray Boyd to tell him that a personal matter required urgent attention and he hoped to be back within ten hours. He then called his DART partner, Brent, to take over the rescue and search coordination until he returned.

Dan was about to leave when Amy emphatically told him she was coming with him. Lillian refused and told her it was far too dangerous; she was far too young but Amy refused to listen to her grandmother. Dan shrugged his shoulders. "I'll look after her, Mrs. Brinkworth—don't worry."

Shortly after ten, they headed to the outskirts of Victoria to pick up the N1 North highway. Dan drove as fast as he could, encountering very few cars on the road. Soon they were approaching the Malahat mountain pass and the apprehension of uncharted territory, plus the seriousness of Paul Brinkworth's plight, reflected eerily on their faces in the soft glow of the dash light.

The drive to Nanaimo produced numerous obstacles that slowed them down, sometimes almost to a standstill, as Dan deviated to avoid large rocks that had been thrown across the road. A few areas in the Malahat had suffered rockslides but several vehicles had braved the debris strewn mountain pass, each having followed the tracks of its predecessor.

Four hours after leaving the Brinkworth home, they were drawing close to their destination. The onramp to the Duke Point ferry appeared in the pickup's lights and it was clear that the overpass had collapsed during the quake. Dan drove carefully up the ramp and onto the Duke Point highway. Another half hour later he saw the

HARMAC junction that led to the large operating pulp mill outside the city of Nanaimo.

Dan knew the area reasonably well. There was a turn off on the road that led to an old deserted mill, the first to be started in the Nanaimo area and this, he believed, was the mill the person mentioned in the text.

They drove down the road to the old mill and on arrival Dan looked for a place to park the pickup where it couldn't be seen by anyone entering the grounds. He soon found a wooded area that provided cover and parked.

Sultan started whining for attention so they got out of the pickup to stretch their legs.

"I wonder who is threatening my Dad. I didn't know he had enemies," mused Amy.

"We'll soon find out," said Dan quietly.

Amy twirled a lock of hair with her fingers. "We don't even have a gun, or anything—how are we going to save him?"

"We don't need a gun," said Dan matter-of-factly. "We have Sultan."

"How can he help us?" she asked, showing a glimmer of a smile at the thought of a dog being a weapon.

"He is combat trained. It's kind of a hobby of mine," said Dan. "I need a pee—wait here."

Disposing of Unwanted Cargo.
Wednesday, 4:50 a.m. 27th September.

The storeroom door swung open with a creak. The sudden noise shattered the barrier of exhausted unconsciousness that had held Paul in its grip through the long night. In an instant he was awake. Gus stood, glaring at him. "Time to go, Brinkworth."

He took a step forward and grabbed Paul's arm, lifting him easily to his feet before bending down to cut the cable tie holding Paul's feet together. Rushmore stood at the entrance, looking impassively at him and with that thin smile that passed as veneer for humor, said, "I enjoyed the company of your girlfriend last night—she's really something."

Paul felt the anger explode within him and tried to lunge at Rushmore, however, a dizzy spell overtook him and fell flat on his face. The fatigue, the beating by O'Kelly, and being trussed up with his hands behind his back had all taken their toll.

Rushmore feigned a look of concern. "Not feeling that well today? Well, don't worry—I have a refreshing experience waiting for you." Paul scrambled to get back on his feet but only succeeded in falling again. Gus helped him up, shoving him toward the back door. A hint of first light was starting in the sky toward the east.

To his surprise the Jeep was parked close by with the engine idling. The vehicle's backdoor was open and he could see a figure bundled in a blanket, sitting very still on the seat; his heart gave a jump—Angeline. What had Rushmore done to her?

His only hope for this world was Rushmore's accomplice, the woman O'Kelly had mentioned—Hilda.

**

Wednesday, 5:10 a.m. 27th September.

Dan watched the lights of two vehicles approaching the old mill's parking area. He glanced at his watch: 5:10 a.m. Amy was asleep so he waited for the vehicles to come to a standstill. Sultan's ears perked straight up. Dan softly gave him a command to be silent and the dog lay down but remained alert.

He then woke Amy up. "They're here. Please stay in the vehicle and don't make a sound," he commanded her sternly. Her eyes opened wide with fright.

"Where are you going," she asked nervously.

"I'm going to find out who it is and see what can be done—I'll take Sultan with me, so be very quiet. If I need you, I will call."

Amy nodded her agreement. Dan called softly to Sultan and they left the vehicle. The night sky glowed with the light of a million stars; the moon, high in the heavens, cast its glow over the deserted mill as the sun slowly started to rise, bringing first light over the waking world of Vancouver Island.

The Northumberland Channel lay shining incandescently, painting an idyllic picture of peace and tranquility.

Dan walked with the dog at his heels until he came around the north corner of the mill. The two vehicles were parked on the wharf facing the strait and two men stood a few feet from the vehicle closest to the water, engaged in earnest conversation. Feeling uncertain as to what course of action to follow, he crouched and waited, whispering for Sultan to lie next to him.

One of the men got back into what appeared to be a Jeep while the other man, holding a revolver in his hand, looked on. The driver started the vehicle and moved slowly toward the edge of the wharf.

Fear gripped Dan's heart when he realized there were people sitting in the rear seat. It became suddenly clear to him what the two men were planning for their captives.

A conflict raged in his mind as he thought of the fate of the people in the Jeep. If he launched an attack now the man with the revolver could pick him off before he covered the distance. Even Sultan would not be able to breach the gap quickly enough.

As the vehicle reached the wharf the driver slid out of the driver's seat and jumped onto the ground leaving the Jeep teetering on the edge. There was a scraping sound as the under-carriage of the vehicle caught the lip of the wharf before toppling six feet into the inky-black water with a loud splash, followed by a dull hiss of compressed air.

The two men peered down at the large bubbles escaping from the vehicle marking the beginning of its slow slide downward toward a watery grave.

Dan sat in stony silence, willing the two men to move on. He desperately wanted to make a rescue attempt on the ill-fated occupants. Uncertain as to the depth of the water next to the wharf, he judged it to be thirty to forty feet.

If it became possible to get into the water without being seen, he might have a chance of diving onto the back of the sinking vehicle. Even a strong swimmer would struggle in water verging on the fall temperatures, radically reducing the time for a rescue.

He remembered Amy had said there were two prisoners—to rescue even one of them under the present conditions would take a miracle.

The two men looked at each other and made a silent gesture of acceptance that their work was done. They started to walk in the direction of the old buildings.

Dan spent an agonizing minute waiting for the men to disappear from view. When he was satisfied they could no longer see the wharf, he ran to the edge and peered down into the dark water. Bubbles of air continued in a long stream, bursting intermittently as they reached the surface.

He quickly kicked off his boots and gave Sultan a command to stay on the wharf, then launched himself into the cold, murky waters. The dog strutted up and down, whining anxiously as he watched his master disappear beneath the surface.

*

Paul Brinkworth could not get Angeline to look at him. Gus had zip-tied his ankles before bundling him into the backseat and strapping him in with the seatbelt. He had moved up next to her as close as he could, trying to look into her eyes but she ignored him completely, seemingly not knowing who he was.

Wrapped in the blanket and totally unresponsive, her eyes stared vacantly at the ceiling. A swelling had appeared above one eye and there was bruising beneath the other; her lips were slightly swollen and cut. It appeared that whatever Rushmore had done to her, she had been completely traumatized.

Escape was out of the question. He thought of Hilda's undertaking to call Megan and wondered if she had been able to make contact. Would Megan be able to marshal help in time to save them?

Everything looked extremely bleak and he prayed a silent prayer for help as the Jeep sped quietly along the highway. Behind them he could just make out the van, driven by Rushmore. A few minutes later they pulled off the highway onto a bumpy, little-used road and after a short distance the vehicle came to a standstill.

Gus got out of the Jeep and walked to where Rushmore stood. Paul couldn't turn his neck to see them clearly but he heard their voices. He started to panic—if there was no intervention now, it could be the end.

After a minute, Gus returned and slid behind the wheel but left the Jeep's door open. He engaged the drive and the Jeep moved slowly forward. Paul wondered what was going on until the Jeep's front end suddenly dipped and slid forward with a sickening lurch. Gus had jumped clear as the Jeep slipped over the edge of the wharf.

Desperately struggling one last time with the zip-tie around his wrists, Paul knew instinctively his captors were going to drown him. The tie bit deeply into his flesh as he yanked frantically, willing the strong plastic to break, but his efforts came to nothing. The dark waters of the Northumberland Strait closed in over the Jeep and all light disappeared. He had lost the battle. No one had come to intervene and save the two of them. He could feel Angeline's body next to him and again he prayed their deaths would be quick.

Water poured in, swirling and thrusting them against the back incline of the seat.

The Jeep took only minutes to settle on the bottom of the channel, thirty feet below the surface. The pressure in Paul's ears increased and his lungs silently screamed for oxygen. His hands, tied behind his back, searched in one last effort for the seatbelt clasp and found it. He poked at the red plastic in the center of the clasp and felt the belt release. His body, suddenly freed up, shot to the roof where a small bubble of air remained, the Jeep having settled onto its wheels .

*

The cold water anesthetized Dan's body as he thrust downward in the wake of the sinking vehicle. It was six months since he had last scuba-dived. What a help it would be to have all my scuba equipment right now, he thought.

The pressure increased in his ears as he pulled himself through the dark, cold water. Instinctively he judged the shift of the Jeep in its downward plunge and blindly thrust on, praying to make contact.

Lungs almost at bursting point and muscles straining, he caught up to the sinking vehicle, his hands crashing into the back door. He banged his head on the window in a frantic bid to find the door's release catch. The Jeep had not yet reached the bottom but was settling like a stricken submarine that had lost all its ballast.

Dan clung desperately to the door-catch housing and with a determined effort managed to press the release mechanism with his thumb. The Jeep settled onto its wheels and for a moment he couldn't budge the door but by bracing his feet on the back bumper he slowly managed to pull it open. A bubble of air trapped against the roof rushed out at him as he lunged into the doomed vehicle feeling wildly around the backseat area.

A body bumped up against Dan's arm and without thinking he grabbed at it.   His ears were becoming extremely painful due to the pressure and he knew he could not remain at that depth for long. With a hefty tug on the inert body it moved toward him and suddenly they were outside the back of the vehicle.

He thrust the body upward toward the vague light of the moonlit sky, then turned to press downward again toward the backdoor of the Jeep. Ninety

219

seconds had elapsed since Dan had entered the water. Little pin-pricks of light danced before his eyes.

There were two people—was the only thought that filled his consciousness. Again, he felt blindly around the backseat area and immediately came across another body which appreared to be wrapped in a blanket. The person's body was fortunately not tied down by a seatbelt so he grabbed onto the head with both hands and pulled with all the dwindling strength he had left, moving backwards toward the open door, then upward, to the faint light above that represented life. The journey to the surface took only a few seconds. As Dan took a life-giving gulp of fresh air he bumped against the body of the first person he had rescued. Noticing that the person was thrashing erratically about he pulled the body towards his own and soon discovered the reason—the person's hands and feet were bound.

∞

Sixteen

A Hopeless Situation.
Wednesday, 5:23 a.m. 27th September.

Paul was on the verge of passing out when he felt something brush against his arm. The next instant he felt a vice-like grip on his shoulder and he was suddenly tugged toward the backdoor. He had not sensed in his befuddled and panicked state that the backdoor was open. A miracle. He was floating quickly upward but realized that the last dregs of air were gone from his lungs; so near and yet so far. Could he make it—he doubted. Images flashed before him. Megan and the kids, his mother, and then his late father. All waved at him, smiling happily, cheering him on, toward some imaginary finishing line.

Strange, he thought. I don't recall entering any race.

And then he burst to the surface and his lungs gulped in huge drafts of air. He was alive. The notion of certain death had become vaguely obscured—only for a brief second, though. He was losing buoyancy, the depths beckoning him again. Hope's silent presence slipped through his grasp like a greasy rope.

*

Amy was feeling anxious about the outcome of Dan's recon and decided to leave the pickup. She justified her actions by thinking she would need to know if her dad was in fact present. After all, Dan had never met her father and would not be able to recognize him. She crept to the nearest wall of the building that housed the old mill and was about to peer round the corner when a rustling of the grass along the pathway caught her attention.

Turning around to stare into the darkness, she was aware of movement in the bushes through which she had just walked. Whoever it was must have been following her footsteps. Not sure if she was hearing things she turned back in the direction she had been walking. Maybe it was Sultan. The noise started again and she knew it had not been her imagination. She stopped again and stared into the shadows.

A deathly quiet reigned for a few seconds until Amy broke it. "Dan—Is that you?"

There was no answer. She called out again but only silence answered. The fear of someone in league with her father's captors was a reality she could not discount.

Suddenly a man's voice shattered the quiet. "Stand still! Don't move or I'll shoot you."

Amy froze. It was not Dan, nor did she recognize the voice.

"Who the hell are you?" asked the voice angrily and the form of a short, stocky man appeared out of the gloom. A strong beam of light dazzled Amy and she took a step backward, raising an arm to shield her eyes.

In fear for her life, Amy remained silent. This was turning out to be a very bad morning.

The man kept the flashlight directed at her face as he approached. He demanded to know what her name was and what she was doing there at that time of the morning.

"My name's Amy," she cried through a deluge of tears.

"Amy who?" The tone of the man's voice reflected his agitation.

Again she remained silent not wanting to give her identity away. The man gave her a shove and she fell to the ground, sobbing.

*

Dan tried to help the person whose hands and feet were bound, to keep their head above water, but trying to hold on to two people and tread was taxing the little strength he had left. He could hear Sultan whining above him on the wharf, anxious to get in and help his master so he gave a low whistle.

The German shepherd launched into the dark waters without reservation and swam toward the three struggling people. When the dog arrived, Dan was desperately trying to keep both people from slipping into the murky depths.

"Save, Sultan...save!" Dan managed to cough out the command, hindered by the need to take breaths of air between each word.

Sultan was in his element. Using his powerful jaws to grab the jacket of the person nearest him, he turned with his cargo in tow and swam toward the wharf.

Realizing there was no place for the dog to disembark, Dan whistled another signal and Sultan turned to head for the adjacent beach of cobbled stones.

He secured his grip on the second person and began to swim slowly, using a crab-like motion, toward the beach—Sultan had already deposited one of the bodies face-down on the gravel, legs extending into the water.

It was a woman. Her ankles and hands were tied with zip-ties and her bedraggled blond hair was plastered against her face. She showed no signs of life. Dan's feet finally touched ground and he waded to where she lay, towing, what appeared to be, the semi-conscious hulk of a man.

Sultan was delighted to see his master and pranced around excitedly, jumping up to lick Dan's face. Dan hauled the man onto the shore and the retrieval part of the rescue was over.

"Good boy, Sultan. You're a good boy!" Dan exclaimed, ecstatic with his canine's first attempt at a real water rescue. The many hours of practice with a dummy in a lake had paid dividends.

"Stand guard, Sultan!"

The dog obediently moved to a point above the beach, a few yards up the path that led to the mill and tested the air with his nose. A scent caught his powerful olfactory senses, causing him to cock his head and stare at the mill building a hundred and fifty feet away. He lay down, keeping an eye on both the building and his master.

Dan hurriedly cut away the zip-ties, holding the woman's hands and feet, with the knife he always kept in the leg pocket of his pants. He started CPR.

The man, lying prone on the cobblestones, spluttered loudly as he regained consciousness. The cold breeze on his wet clothing caused him to shudder violently as feeling started to return to his numbed body.

After a count of twenty chest pumps the woman responded to the CPR. Her eyes flickered open and she regurgitated a mouth full of water. Dan tilted her head to the side to enable the water to escape her throat more easily. He then left her to check on the man who was trying to get himself into a sitting position.

"You are Mr. Brinkworth, I presume?" asked Dan as he cut the zip-ties from Paul's hands and feet.

Paul lay on his back and looked up at his rescuer. "Yes—did my wife send you?"

Dan hesitated for a few seconds before answering. "Not exactly. It was your daughter, Amy."

He proceeded to tell Paul the whole story but was interrupted by violent bouts of throwing-up by the woman who had now rolled onto her side in an attempt to evacuate the remaining seawater from her lungs.

Paul, having recovered sufficiently, sat up with a jerk and peered past Dan.

"Angie—you're alive, thank God."

Dan helped Paul onto his feet and they moved to Angeline's side. Paul wrapped his arms around her and for a few moments he continued to embrace her cold, shivering body against his own.

She remained silent and unresponsive.

Dan put his hand on Paul's shoulder. "She's in deep shock, Mr. Brinkworth. I need to get blankets from my pickup for both of you."

After commanding Sultan to stay, Dan left Paul and Angeline sitting on the cobblestones and ran toward the buildings, behind which lay the grass path, leading to the pickup.

Arriving at the truck, he called to Amy, but there was no answer. Maybe she got bored and wondered off to investigate the buildings. Dan pulled out the blankets and his backpack.

His arrival at the beach was heralded with a few short barks from Sultan, who pranced around his master, with much whining and tail wagging.

Paul and Angeline were now sitting apart from one another and it was apparent that shock had set in with both. Dan quickly threw blankets around them and took out his thermos from the backpack. The coffee was still steaming in the cool atmosphere of the early morning. The first rays of the sun breached the horizon and the stars were fading into the dawning sky.

Paul was the first to speak, his voice shaky from the effects of delayed shock. "You didn't...finish... telling me how you found...us."

Dan repeated what he had told Paul initially, plus the news of Meg's accident and Amy's desperate call to him the previous evening. He ended the story with how he had watched the Jeep go over the edge of the wharf–"and here we are, cold...in shock, but alive."

Angeline was a little more responsive, making eye contact with Dan, but not Paul.

Paul sensed her reluctance to deal with what Rushmore had done to her. All he could do was take her hand and stroke it, not asking any questions. It could wait.

Paul asked the inevitable question. "Where's my daughter? You mentioned she came with you."

Dan frowned and said, "I don't know where she is. I left her in the pickup and told her not to leave but when I returned for the blankets she was gone."

"Maybe she's checking out the buildings. Perhaps I had better look for her," said Paul, slowly trying to get up.

Dan put out a restraining hand and stood to his feet. "You are in no condition to do anything just yet—wait here and rest up for a bit longer. I'll have a quick look to see if I can find her."

Suddenly Sultan stiffened and released a low growl that emanated from the back of his throat.

Dan turned and stared at the ridge of ground between them and the row of derelict buildings.

The heads of two men appeared, and then a third, that of a young girl. The girl was sandwiched between the men and as they drew closer Paul recognized them—Rushmore and Gus; between them was his daughter Amy. In that moment he hit rock bottom.

*

The man helped the terrified teenage girl to her feet. "I won't hurt you if you tell me what you are doing here."

Amy knew she could not divulge her true identity as it would put her father and Dan at further risk. She lied off the cuff. "I came down here to do some bird watching. My father is fishing close by."

The man looked at her suspiciously. "Bird watching? There are no birds to see at this time of the morning—you're a lying little bitch!"

Amy broke down into tears again and said, "Please don't hurt me. I'm not lying to you."

"Come with me," he said without further ado. "We'll see what the boss-man says."

Amy was marched down the path and through the bushes until they came to the road that led to the old mill. The man jerked her roughly in the direction of a building where a van was parked and called out to a man sitting in the passenger seat.

"It's a young girl—she was snooping around the corner of the end building."

The other man opened the door of the van and stepped onto the ground. He was tall, slender, and softly spoken. "We saw you walking through the bushes and wondered what on earth you were doing out here at this time. What's your name, sweetheart?" His voice sounded like the hiss of a cobra.

"My name's Amy," she said hesitantly.

"Are you alone?" he asked, peering into her eyes.

"No. I told this man that my dad is fishing nearby and I wanted to do some bird watching."

The taller man laughed. "Yeah, right—like I'm here to sample the air."

Amy said nothing. A look of embarrassment crept over her pretty features, knowing she was a terrible liar.

"You will tell me the truth or I will allow this ugly man to remove all your clothes," the tall man said.

The threat had an obvious meaning and for a fourteen year old there was nothing worse.

Amy tried to jerk her arm from the short man's grip but he was too strong. He held her close to him and she could smell his breath as he brought his face close to hers.

"Well...are you going to tell us why you're here or do I get to do what this man suggested?"

Frightened out of her wits, Amy blurted out the truth and hated herself for it. Starting with the strange text received, she related the entire story of the call to Dan and the decision to help her father.

Rushmore was particularly interested in hearing about the text. "Did this person give a name?"

Amy blinked and looked away. "No— but it was sent from my dad's phone."

Rushmore and Gus looked at each other and then slowly nodded their heads in agreement.

The taller man smiled and said, "I thought there was some connection—so you're Brinkworth's daughter?"

She nodded and started sobbing.

He looked at the shorter man and said, "This actually works in our favor, Gus. There is only one other person who had access to that phone—Hilda, and if this guy, Dan, has been hero enough to rescue Brinkworth and his girlfriend, assuming such a rescue was possible, then I think I have the master of all plans."

Gus smiled and stroked Amy's hair. "Don't worry, darling—I don't do little girls," he said soothingly.

The taller man started walking toward the wharf area. "Let's see if your friend 'Dan' has played the hero."

They left the van and trooped around the side of a building toward the waterline, which lay just beyond the high ground, obscuring the wharf area from their sight.

As they reached the ridge, the adjacent beach came into view and they saw three people seated on the cobblestones, two with blankets draped over them. A large shepherd crouched intimidatingly on the path in front of them, head lowered and teeth bared. A low, deep growl warned the intruders they should not get too close.

Rushmore and Gus, who held Amy in front of him, walked cautiously to within twenty feet of the dog before coming to a halt. Sultan immediately took two steps forward and increased the intensity of his growling.

Dan stood slowly to his feet and was the first to speak. "Are you okay, Amy?"

Paul remained silent and Angeline looked away, to the gathering light in the eastern sky.

Rushmore raised the revolver and aimed it threateningly at the dog. "Call off your animal or I'll put a bullet in him."

It seemed a one-sided stand-off to Dan so he gave Sultan a command to break off the engagement. The dog instantly obeyed and sat, but remained between the two groups.

Paul said, "What do you intend to do, Rushmore?"

"I'm not sure how this rescue was pulled off but it doesn't really change anything. I could kill all four of you but I have a better plan—if you want to listen that is."

"Go ahead," said Paul, feeling there was nothing to lose.

Rushmore lowered the gun as if in a gesture of goodwill. In reality, with the ferry across the fence line, four gun shots would attract attention even this early in the morning. "We are going to keep your daughter with us, Brinkworth. She will be our insurance against your running off to the authorities regarding our little caper in the rainforest."

"I can't allow that," Paul said quickly.

"You actually have no option, Brinkworth. We're holding the aces and if you don't comply, all of you will die."

Paul did not know what to say.

"I assure you no harm will come to your daughter while she's in our care. There might also be something in it for you and we can work out how your daughter can be returned."

Paul and Dan looked at each other. Dan shrugged his shoulders and said, "It's up to you, Mr. Brinkworth. At this moment I don't see that we have much choice."

Paul looked at the ground, then at Angeline who continued to gaze at the sky, as if she were not there.

Then he looked at his daughter. "Don't worry, baby. I will work this out and you'll be back home soon."

Amy sobbed, overwhelmed at the sight of her bedraggled-looking father and did not want to accept that she could not go to him.

Rushmore looked at Dan. "I assume it's your pickup parked behind the buildings under the trees?"

Dan nodded.

"Mr. Brinkworth, I want you to pay me a visit at my home, as soon as possible." Rushmore looked directly at Paul. "You'll find the details in the phone book under B. Rushmore. We can discuss terms regarding the return of your daughter, but if you try anything, you will never see her again—is that understood?"

Paul glanced quickly at Dan and then back at Rushmore. "If you as much as harm one hair on her head, I swear, I'll hunt you down and kill you. You have made yourself clear and I hope I have done the same."

Rushmore half turned, looked at Dan, and then raised the gun to Amy's head. "Keep that beast of yours away from us."

He looked at Paul again. "I am in the phone book, Brinkworth. I will expect a visit from you on your return to Victoria. In the meantime, I will take good care of your very pretty little girl."

With that the two men started toward the line of buildings. Amy protested violently, trying to wrench herself free from their grasp and screamed for her father to help her. Paul's heart broke to see them cart her off but he had no other choice. He felt helpless and for the moment dropped his head as the tears flowed down his cheeks.

Angeline stood slowly and unsteadily to her feet. She moved to Paul and put her arms around him but said nothing. They embraced each other while Dan looked on, perplexed.

Sultan looked to his master for a signal but there was none forthcoming so he sat and cocked his head in a quizzical fashion.

They stood for an interminable time before Paul released his embrace of Angeline and looked at Dan.

"We need to get back to Victoria—there's nothing more to be done here."

Dan nodded in agreement and they slowly made their way to the pickup.

∞

Seventeen

Coordinating Emergency Assistance.
Wednesday, 10:00 a.m. 27th September.

Bud Hamlin stood at the corner of Dallas and Montreal streets in Victoria, surveying the destruction. The air was cold and still with the cerulean sky reflecting brightly on the waters of the Juan De Fuca Strait.

The aftermath of the quake was into its third day. Reports pouring in from the various relief centers overshadowed those of any previous disaster Bud had witnessed or read about.

The death toll reached four thousand and rose steadily every hour as news came in from various sources.

The area he surveyed was a large contributor to that figure. Drowned bodies of pedestrians and residents were discovered every ten minutes.

Bud returned to his vehicle and drove slowly through the empty neighborhood. Stopping every now and then, he made notes on a piece of paper clamped on a yellow clipboard. As the local director of Emergency Preparedness Canada, he needed to have a firsthand knowledge of the state of the city.

Smoke from dozens of fires, some already burned out, hung like a heavy blanket over most of the city. It could have been a scene from one of the many war torn areas of the third world.

He continued on his fact-finding mission. The DART teams had performed well. Reports of many heroic acts were flowing in, bringing perspective on injuries and fatalities.

The Department of National Defense in Ottawa had been contacted and help was on its way. The federal government had previously established a large unit of firefighters, soldiers, and engineers in Alberta to help with disasters in western Canada.

The radio came to life every few seconds with characteristic static sounds as messages were relayed between various members of the response teams. Tuning briefly to another frequency Bud picked up a broadcast from Vancouver:

"...Head of the Provincial Emergency Program in Vancouver, Brian Mason, has declared a state of emergency in British Columbia. Relief from the federal government's Earthquake Support Plan has started to pour into the province... "

Satisfied that help would soon be on its way for the island, he returned to the emergency channel.

Wednesday, 10:30 a.m. 27th September.

Cleanup teams had been mobilized by the Greater Victoria District to clear up the worst of the highways. Dangerous areas had been cordoned off, and huge trucks working with loaders were busy removing rubble from collapsed overpasses.

Paul, Angeline, and Dan arrived in Victoria mid-morning. Their first port of call was the Victoria General Hospital where Angeline was checked in for a quick examination of her injuries and an evaluation of overall condition. The doctor in emergency wanted her to stay overnight to ensure she was on the road to recovery.

Paul and Dan then left for the Saanich Peninsula Hospital where they met a tearful Lillian Brinkworth and a boisterous Jason, waiting for an opportunity to see Meg. Lillian wanted to know where Amy was and he told her Amy had stayed with some people in Nanaimo and would be home soon. He promised to explain later.

The family sat around Meg's hospital bed. She was festooned with drips and tubes, a heart monitor, and other medical paraphernalia. Before entering her ward, they spent fifteen minutes with

238

the chief of surgery, a Dr. Scott, who briefed them on Megan's condition.

"She's not out of danger yet. We also can't tell if she will make a full recovery."

The words floated in the back of Paul's mind as he watched Meg's pale, expressionless face. He realized how much he loved her; the thought of losing her love and companionship brought a huge lump to his throat. Not to ever see her beautiful face again would be the greatest punishment of his lifetime.

He thought of Angeline and guilt, born from their passion that early morning in the mountain pass, haunted him unmercifully. He knew he had to see Angeline soon and end the affair, but an emotion, deep inside was not responding to the severing of the relationship. She had crept into his heart, a truth he could not deny. She was also in a very frail state of mind at the present—a sudden break-off by him might shatter the hopes of any recovery from her terrible ordeal at the hands of Rushmore.

These thoughts, and the endurance of their recent life-threatening circumstances, seemed to justify a need for each other. In some way he felt they had earned the right to a relationship. As much as he tried to entertain this line of thought, integrity railed against it.

Later that afternoon, Lillian and Jason returned to the family home while Paul opted to remain at the hospital with his wife. Dan stayed for an hour and then left to feed Sultan who had not eaten for at least twenty-four hours. The two men were now on first name terms and had become firm friends.

Paul stayed at the bedside talking softly to Meg, holding her limp hand in his, but she remained unresponsive. After two more hours he decided to go home, shower, and have a night's rest. The fate of his daughter rested heavily upon his shoulders and he knew sleep was going to be evasive.

**

Wednesday, 3:05 p.m. 27th September.

On their return to Nanaimo, Rushmore and Gus left Amy at a house that served as a storage facility for the Hurricane Charley product plus varieties of bathroom fresheners.

A stern, lugubrious woman was in charge of the house and looked after the inventory. She also cleaned the place and maintained the garden outside. A room in the basement which had a high, barred window was Amy's prison for the foreseeable future and was decked out with a single bed, en-suite bathroom, television, plus plenty of magazines scattered for her to read.

He shoved Amy into the room and barked an instruction to the woman, "Rose—see that the girl is fed and looked after until I come again. Don't let her out of the room—it may be a little while."

The woman nodded and stared at Amy through the steel gate that took the place of a door to the room.

Rushmore abruptly turned on his heel and left for the shop at Woodgrove Center.

On arrival at the shop, Rushmore called Hilda aside and said, "Let's get some lunch."

She was nervous and asked him if the plan had succeeded, to which he replied, "It's done, don't worry about it."

They left for the food court, which since the earthquake, only had three vendors operating. There were only a few people around, checking out what shops were open. Rushmore ordered sushi with Hilda opting for a Greek salad from Opa's. After retrieving their respective meals, they sat at one of the many tables in the court.

Hilda felt edgy but was confident that Rushmore could not know about the text she sent Brinkworth's wife. Rushmore seemed in a pleasant mood and indulged in small talk about the quake and the condition of their surroundings. When they finished eating, Rushmore leaned back in the seat and said, "So, I believe you sent Brinkworth's wife a text."

Hilda froze.

Rushmore continued, "Don't worry—nothing came of it. I can understand that you have some reservations about my style of handling things but you really need to trust me. I know what is best and I hope I can gain your respect for that."

Hilda did not know what to say and looked embarrassed.

"There won't be another opportunity so I hope you'll toe the line in future. You owe me."

Hilda was quiet for a moment then answered. "Thank you, Barry. I guess I got scared. It won't happen again; are we okay?"

"That depends," he said with a smirk, the tiny blue and purple lines in his face appeared exaggerated as he craned forward to stare into her face. His cold, calculating blue eyes searched the depths of her self-confidence and she felt uneasy. Rushmore was not a person to play games.

He looked at her, licking his bottom lip and she immediately understood what he meant. She was being asked to offer herself, her body for restitution. This did not particularly worry her—after all, virtue and honor had been lost a long time ago. Self-respect would have to be measured against survival. What did worry her was his kinky, sexual practices but there was no way out of his net.

He continued to stare at her for a while before lowering his gaze to below her neckline. She nodded her head slightly in acceptance of his obvious intentions and they left the restaurant. Rushmore drove her to a secluded spot at Ten Mile Point, a neighborhood in the district of Saanich and parked the car on a knoll overlooking the sea—accept for a few seagulls and the sound of waves, they were completely alone.

They transferred to the car's plush backseat after Rushmore had taken a thick towel from the trunk. He laid the towel on the backseat and they proceeded to remove clothing. Settling down together, in not the most comfortable of positions, Rushmore made his advance on her.

Hilda opened herself, hesitantly at first to his probing hands, believing that giving herself to him was a necessary sacrifice to secure his good graces. She thought he would want to keep her around for a while if she could fulfill his desires and then he would lose interest.

Rushmore, however, had other plans. Alarm suddenly filled Hilda's thoughts as she felt his hands close on her throat. Then a wild panic set in as Rushmore began to choke her, all the while looking intently into her eyes. Suddenly he released his grip and slapped her face as hard as he could. She briefly lost consciousness.

After he abused her body for several minutes, satisfying his deranged sexual drive, he reached into the pocket on the back of the front passenger seat and pulled out a knife. Hilda partially regained consciousness and was lying beneath him. With her head turned away—she never saw the quick

243

movement of his hand as he plunged the knife into her neck.

He lay quietly looking at her as she passed, a thin smile dawning fleetingly on his otherwise impassive face. He raised himself off of her body and grabbed up the thick towel that draped the seat underneath them to soak up the blood that had escaped the artery in her final moments.

He wrapped the towel around her neck and shoulders, making sure no blood dripped onto the leather seat and carried her body into the bushes at the periphery of the parking area.

After he dumped her, he searched her purse and pulled out a small notebook. From his jacket, lying on the front seat, he took a pen and made a brief notation in the notebook before returning it to her purse. He glanced once more at the body and dumped the purse next to it.

Finally, with a quick glance around the area to satisfy himself that no one had witnessed the murder, Rushmore drove away.

**

Thursday, 8:00 a.m. 28th September.

Paul needed to do several things, now that he was home again. The first was to tell his mother what was going on; not the full version, but particularly that Amy wouldn't be home for a while. The difficult part was to display confidence that his daughter's predicament was temporary. He did not want his mother running off to the police and endangering Amy's position.

He also had to report Tom Wilson's death to the police and the whereabouts of the body—it would get too complicated if he tried to tell the police the whole truth. He had discussed the problem with Dan and they decided it would be wise to allow events to unfold as time went on. Paul had to ensure Amy's safety before they could think of how to deal with Rushmore. When she was out of harm's way they would see what options remained open. He also needed to visit Gertrude Wilson, Tom's wife.

Lillian Brinkworth was not fooled by her son's brief explanation of events but had the presence of mind not to press the issue. She realized nothing would be accomplished by badgering him, and if he was going to report it to the police, things would get sorted out. She retired to the guest bedroom to pray like any devout Christian would. Paul borrowed his mother's car and drove to the Victoria central police offices where he reported the matter of Tom Wilson's death to a disinterested duty officer.

The duty officer quickly told him, "There isn't anything I can do from here. I will report it to the police in Port Alberni—that's their jurisdiction.

What I will do, however, is send an officer to see Mrs. Wilson and inform her of her husband's death. It's standard procedure."

She wrote down the particulars, not even raising an eyebrow at the fact that a murder had been committed.

Paul asked her for a phone book which she dutifully grabbed from beneath the counter and placed in front of him, before turning her back to answer the phone.   He quickly looked up Rushmore's details and discovered there were three in the book but only one B. Rushmore, an address in Gordon's Head.

It was an hour drive to Rushmore's home. Perhaps not surprisingly, the beautiful house sat on an acre of ground in close proximity to where his parents had once lived, before his father had passed away.

The gardens were professionally landscaped and swept to the boundaries. The grass lawns were neatly trimmed at the edges and imported exotic bushes framed the mansion, giving the impression of wealth.

Paul parked his mother's car in front of the main entrance and tentatively stepped onto the driveway. The window drapes were all drawn, giving the place a deserted look. He walked to the front door and rang the doorbell a few times until a sulky young girl answered. She appeared to have just woken up.

He wondered what sort of night life she led, sleeping at that time of the day.

"Is Mr. Rushmore in?"

"My step-father's out at the moment. I think he's gone up to Nanaimo."

"When will he be back?" asked Paul.

The young girl yawned cavernously and spoke at the same time. "He said he'd be back tonight, but it depended on his business.   Shall I tell him you called? Who shall I say...?"

Paul thought quickly. "Tell him Paul Brinkworth dropped by—I will come again tomorrow morning."

She nodded and closed the door, leaving him standing. He stared at the door handle for a moment and then walked back to the car.

*

Later that afternoon Paul drove to the Wilson's home. Upon his arrival at the house he knocked on the door. It was answered immediately by a short, middle-aged woman. She did not smile and her eyes were swollen with dark underlying rings. Her stooping frame exuded sorrow and a tear-soaked handkerchief was twirled nervously through thin, sensitive fingers.

"I'm looking for Gertrude Wilson...is she in?"

"Gertrude was badly injured in the earthquake and is in hospital," the woman answered dabbing her eyes with the handkerchief. "I'm Gladys, Gertrude's older sister—I'm looking after the children. Please come in."

"Did the police call about Tom?" Paul asked pensively.

"Are you Paul Brinkworth?"

"Yes."

"The police said you would be able to give us some details..."

Paul nodded. "I was with him when it happened...shall we sit and talk?"

The meeting with Gertrude's sister took only thirty minutes. Paul discovered Gertrude had not yet been told about her husband's death. The pastor of the church they attended had been called and would break the news when her condition was more stable.

Paul still felt an obligation to share the details with her when she returned home. Finally he left the Wilson homestead and wanting to be with Meg, he headed for the Saanich Peninsula again. There had been no change in her condition.

∞

Eighteen

Dealing with the Devil.
Friday, 9:35 a.m. 29th September.

The next morning Paul drove back to Rushmore's house and parked the car in the driveway. Rushmore's daughter answered the doorbell promptly. She glared at him for a moment before inviting him into the expensively furnished living room.

"My step-father will be with you in a few minutes."

She lingered for a moment to see if Paul wanted to say anything and then trudged upstairs to her bedroom. Paul took mental note of the décor as Rushmore's expensive taste became evident. Original paintings hung on the walls and eighteenth century styled furnishings occupied the living room floor. Over the back of a petite settee, draped an exquisite quilt with embellished ruffles; across the room, a partial quilt project hung over a wooden frame.

Rushmore entered and the two men stared at each other. Rushmore nodded and motioned for Paul to be seated.

"So, Brinkworth—have you thought about the status quo?"

Paul nodded but remained quiet.

Rushmore continued, "I think you have realized that I don't fuck around when I put my mind to something, however, I have always considered myself to be a fair man."

"Go on." Paul's voice was barely audible.

Rushmore examined his fingernails and continued. "Our operation in the forest, as you no doubt know, produces a drug called Hurricane Charley. The operation has been active for several years and started with a grow-op but got elevated to H.C. when marijuana was medically legalized. We discovered marijuana's street value diminished over a short period of time after that, but H.C. has turned over a handsome profit since its inception two years ago. There are some extremely powerful, well-connected political entities involved so if you think you are up to taking on this cartel, you would be more than a brave man."

Paul glowered at Rushmore, wishing he could grab the man and throttle him but kept his peace.

"If you're as clever as I think you are, you will consider the odds to be hugely against you and your friends, however, if you decide to get involved with us, you could end up a very rich man."

"What you're saying is that you are blackmailing me and the others into being your fucking pawns," Paul growled.

"I guess you could say that but then again, it depends how you look at it. There is no place for heroes in this world, Brinkworth. People only respond to money."

"Life is not all about money, Rushmore—it's about living life with integrity."

"Sure, sure...I've heard it all. You can be a poor hero or a rich citizen; the choice is yours," Rushmore returned with his thin, veneer of a smile. "You can be a poor hero with all your integrity but you will also have a daughter who will be sold into prostitution in some foreign country and you will never find her."

The words confirmed Paul's worst fears about Rushmore. He was a ruthless son-of-a-bitch who didn't care about anyone but himself.

He knew he had to comply for the moment; it appeared Rushmore was going to offer him an alternative and as long as he kept his wits about him Amy would be safe for the time being.

"What are you offering, Rushmore? Whatever it is, you know I will always consider you to be a bastard."

"I don't give a shit what you think of me, Brinkworth. We can end up helping each other in the long run and you will save the life of your daughter. Just remember, if the people involved with H.C. feel threatened in any way, they will quickly instruct me to take out your family—one by one, starting with your young son and you will be last. Your choice is a simple one."

Paul went cold at the mention of Jason.

"Talk and you will jeopardize the lives of your family, especially your pretty teenage daughter—keep your mouth shut and we might be able to find a way to keep her...pure."

Paul was stunned into silence as he considered what Rushmore was saying. The enormity of the situation suddenly became apparent and he wilted into the chair like a man who just received a death sentence.

His anger suddenly turned to fear. For a brief moment he thought he was going to be sick, and Rushmore, sensing his confusion, piled on the pressure.

"We also know that your wife Megan is still in the hospital...a vulnerable place to be, don't you think?"

The use of the family names personified the threat. Rushmore had obviously done his homework on the Brinkworth family. The fact they knew about his wife's hospitalization showed a determination to push home their advantage, regardless of the cost involved.

"Your very accommodating reporter girlfriend also needs to be warned." A glare twinkled in

Rushmore's eye. "Tell me, Paul. Does Megan know you've 'taken a dip' into forbidden land? I must agree, the little whore is as beautiful as she tastes."

Paul stared at him stonily.

Rushmore's face glazed over for a moment then turned hard. "I don't know how much she knows, but we'll hold you responsible for anything she reports."

Paul remained silent, staring at Rushmore through narrowed eyelids and did his best to keep his composure. He needed to be alone, to think this through. Revulsion for Rushmore was growing by the second and the impulse to strangle him on the spot was interfering with his ability to approach the matter rationally.

With extreme self-control, Paul rose from the chair and with a murderous glare at Rushmore, he walked to the front door and let himself out.

Rushmore raised his voice. "Don't forget what I said about the girlfriend! If you want to do a deal including her, let me know. I'm sure after some consideration you'll see everything in a different light."

Paul walked to the car, his nerves at breaking point and close to tears. The first thing he needed was to find a place he could relax and think.

There had to be something he could do to extricate himself and his family from this nightmare.

*

When Paul arrived home it was already past midday. Lillian had prepared lunch, which she left in the microwave. He ate half, but struggled with the nausea that gripped the pit of his stomach.

He retired to his bathroom and absentmindedly turned on the cold water, staring at the tiny trickle of brown fluid that emerged. The service had not yet been restored and he cursed the earthquake, the authorities, and the circumstances. Running fingers through his greasy hair he stared at the haggard reflection in the mirror. Fortunately they had a rainwater tank outside, still reasonably full. The winter rains had filled it to overflowing but much had been used on the garden during the hot summer months.

Paul drew water, using a large plastic container and carted it to the bathroom in preparation of a cold wash. When that had been accomplished he settled down in the study to see if the internet was up and running. The service was still down so he went up to the bedroom and lay down on the bed to think.

The double bed seemed suddenly very big and lonely without Meg. He thought of his comatose wife and his daughter, the prisoner of a psychopath, wondering if there would ever be peace in his home again. His tortured mind, trying desperately to escape the reality of the threat against him wanted to shut out the world, but Amy's pretty face kept appearing before him like a sweet angel, pleading with her large blue eyes. She had her mother's hair and complexion—he could not stem the longing in his heart to hold them.

After half an hour of torturous mind games, he began to think more objectively about their plight, allowing his thoughts to roam over any possibility that presented itself. Finding a weakness in Rushmore's corrupt fortress was imperative.

An idea dawned. Eventually the hint of a smile broke out on his face and he whispered softly, "That might just work."

After setting his alarm clock for four p.m., he fell into a fitful sleep.

**

Friday, 5:00 p.m. 29th September.

Paul sat at a restaurant table opposite Angeline and ordered coffee. Every detail of the conversation with Rushmore was still fresh in his mind. However, the idea that had come to him earlier had inspired him to believe there was a possible way out of the predicament.

Angeline was subdued and kept looking at her shaking hands folded in her lap. She wanted to cry continuously. The doctor had prescribed medication for post-traumatic stress disorder saying she would need to find suitable counseling for her mental condition—her boss, Andrew Mortimer, had given her two weeks off to recover from the ordeal.

Paul was acutely aware of her fragile condition but he desperately needed her help.

"I need to take you into full confidence. Our very lives depend on following the plan I'm about to share with you, but you must promise to cooperate all the way with me, particularly when it comes to reporting news concerning that illegal operation we discovered."

She remained silent but nodded that she was listening.

"I know you have been through a terrible ordeal and I wish I could have prevented it. I hope that one day you will forgive me for not saving you from that monster."

She looked surprised at his confession and answered, "Paul, I will never blame you for anything. I know there was nothing you could have done about Rushmore. You did rescue me from that terrible side-kick of O'Kelly's. I will never forget that." She reached out and took his hand.

Paul felt a huge lump in his throat as he tried to find words that would adequately express his feelings.

She waited for him to overcome the emotion that prevented him from talking.

A minute of embarrassing silence passed before he finally found his tongue again. "Let me tell you what has just transpired and then I will tell you what I think we should do."

He poured his heart out regarding the mornings meeting with Rushmore, the danger it posed to his family, to her, and Dan. Then he shared the details of the plan he had come up with and when he finished, he breathlessly sat back and waited for her to absorb the realities.

Angeline considered the danger of Paul's proposal. "So we have to find out who the main players in this operation are before we can put your plan into action?"

"Exactly. I think I know how we can do that, but I first have to see Rushmore again and feign my cooperation with their organization."

"Paul..."

"I know, Angie, how you feel—let's talk about us when we're out of this mess."

She nodded and squeezed his hand lightly. A smile blossomed on her lips and the lines of stress seemed to melt from around her eyes, sending Paul's heart running for cover. Once again, moral confusion reigned for a brief moment, but with a concerted effort he put it aside—there was a job to be done.

*

After visiting Meg's bedside that evening, he called Rushmore's home number. There was no answer so he left a voicemail to say he had reconsidered things and would be around in the morning.

Then he called Dan Duplessis. "Dan, we need to discuss an urgent matter."

"What's it about?" Dan asked.

"The need to protect you, Angeline, and my family."

"How can I help?" Dan asked, cautiously.

"What's your home address? I'll come to your place and explain over a cup of coffee."

The South African readily agreed. That evening the two men sat in the living room drinking coffee and talking about the miraculous rescue that Dan had managed to pull off. After Paul had shared the events which had led up to the attempted murder by Rushmore he proceeded to talk about his morning meeting with the drug lord. After bringing Dan up to date, Paul revealed his plan.

"Help me free my family from this evil. We cannot involve the police at this point, not until I can produce enough evidence. Amy's life hangs in the balance—you and Angeline are also in danger."

Dan did not hesitate to respond, "You can count on me, Paul. Just let me know what you want me to do."

Later that evening Paul drove back to his home, feeling that there was a glimmer of hope to hang on to. On arrival, the house was quiet. He thought his mother and Jason would both be in bed but they were waiting up for him, both sitting at the kitchen table. He realized he had spent very little time with his son since returning from up-island, a situation he should immediately rectify. Lillian left the two of them to talk and retired to the guest room.

**

Saturday, 9:30 a.m. 30th September.

Paul pulled into the driveway of the Rushmore residence and parked behind a van belonging to a renovation and repair company, with one of the backdoors left open. The van gave him an idea that would, to some extent, supplement his action plan for the near future. But first Paul had to convince Rushmore he would do anything to protect his own family, even join the illegal drug operation. Because of his hate for Rushmore it was going to be the most difficult thing for him to articulate, but it was the only way forward.

He smiled wryly to himself as he thought of the irony of his actions. He was indeed afraid but would do what had to be done. If the plan worked, Rushmore and his cohorts would never know who betrayed them. The essential evidence still had to be discovered and it was another reason why, after this meeting he had to get back into Rushmore's house, as soon as possible.

Paul was convinced the evidence he needed was somewhere in the study. He had noticed a laptop, filing cabinet, and a locked roll-top desk previously.

Preparing himself mentally, he approached the door to ring the bell, hoping Rushmore was home. Footsteps sounded in the hallway and Rushmore's daughter opened the door.

"Come in. My step-father will be down in a moment."

Paul walked through the hallway into the sitting room and waited. Rushmore appeared with a smug smile, motioning for Paul to be seated.

"So you've changed your mind?"

"Yes, I have, however, I want you to know I hate what you stand for and I am only doing this to protect my family."

"I understand your distaste for our line of work, but in time, if you keep your mouth shut, you may even make some money out of it."

"Look, Rushmore, I don't want to benefit from your illegal operations.   I want to protect my family, so tell me what you want me to do."

"At this point I don't want you to do anything. Just keep your mouth shut. You'll be contacted after the weekend. Did you speak to your girlfriend and the guy who rescued you?"

Paul held Rushmore's intensive gaze. "Yes—they will cooperate. Now, when do I get to see my daughter?"

Rushmore said, "When I say so. You haven't earned any trust yet so we will speak of this again, next week."

"I'm warning you, Rushmore. Touch a hair on her head and all hell will break loose in your fucking life."

"Relax, Brinkworth. I have no intention of harming the girl, however, if I detect that you so much as sneeze in the direction of the police, I will make sure you'll never see her again."

Paul realized he was not helping the cause by making threats. "I understand perfectly, Rushmore—I will keep my side of the deal if you keep yours. You need have no fear of that, however, I need to see she is okay."

"As I said, we'll talk about that next week," said Rushmore, seemingly satisfied. "I have to visit our little site at Tofino tomorrow and see what's left of

261

it, but should be back by the evening. I will contact you Monday, maybe Tuesday."

From where he was sitting, Paul could see through the study's open door. He noticed the filing cabinet next to the desk did not look to be locked and the top drawer had not been completely closed. He was sure the answer to his dilemma lay somewhere in its contents.

He spied a passive infrared monitor in the corner of the room. There were minor cracks running along the walls just below the ceiling line but the house, on the whole, appeared to have survived the earthquake extremely well.

An idea began to formulate in his mind as to how they could gain entrance to the home without raising any suspicions. Dan would be an ideal part of that plan.

The young girl suddenly appeared at the sitting room entrance. "I'm going out with some of my friends."

Rushmore hesitated and then asked, "When will you be back?"

"Later," she answered with a hint of irritation in her tone.

"Make sure you're back by six—and by the way, your mother will be staying in Vancouver for another two days—we can have some fun tonight."

The daughter ignored his attempt at levity and left the room.

Rushmore shook his head and looked at Paul. "Teenagers—they should be living on their own planet."

He stood to indicate the meeting was at an end.

Paul walked to the front door without another word.   ∞

Nineteen

Stealing Information.
Sunday morning, 1st October.

The next morning Dan and Paul took a slow drive to the Rushmore residence in Dan's pickup. On the back, between empty tins of paint, a ladder and workman's toolbox, lay Sultan.

After they had parked, Dan gave the German shepherd an order to stay and stand guard. He then picked up the ladder, together with a tin of paint, and walked around the house to the backdoor. After knocking several times Rushmore's step-daughter appeared bleary-eyed, hair in disarray.

"I didn't think you guy's worked on Sundays," she said with a yawn.

"We have a heavy schedule next week," replied Dan gruffly. The girl looked at him suspiciously.

"Where are the other two men?"

"I've been told to touch up a few areas here in the kitchen and the hallway. They're working on another job."

At a glance he could see how far the workmen had progressed with their paintjob and exactly where they had stopped the previous day.

"I don't know if I should let you in—there's no one home and my step-father never said anything about you people working today. He's been so preoccupied lately so I suppose it slipped his mind."

Dan was prepared for the questions. "We'll really have problems next week if l can't work a few hours this morning."

"Not my problem—fine, whatever. I'm downloading a program onto my computer in my bedroom—so try not to bother me," she said insolently.

"I know what to do so I'll just get on with it—won't bother you at all," answered Dan, containing his irritation at the girl's attitude.

He moved into the kitchen and put the ladder down while the girl opened the refrigerator, helping herself to ice cream and a soda.

Without a glance in Dan's direction she left the kitchen and climbed the stairs. He quickly slipped outside and beckoned Paul to join him, leaving Sultan to stand guard in the back of the pickup.

"He'll bark if anyone comes up the drive," Dan said proudly. "He's my canine warning system."

Paul slipped into Rushmore's office while Dan set up the ladder in the kitchen where he could watch the stairwell. They had a prearranged signal should the girl come out of her room.

The office was neat and tidy. Everything had its place and Rushmore was obviously a man who was well organized. The filing cabinet was unlocked so Paul checked over the neatly typed file headings. One caught his eye immediately: 'HCharley.'

He pulled out the folder and checked the contents. There were lists of products under names such as 'Bath Salt Glamor' and 'Soapy Salt Fresh,' each of these showing the numbers of bottles manufactured, aligned with dates. Paul was thrilled to have found a connection to the drug operation, however, he quickly realized it was not sufficient evidence to build a case.

Rushmore's laptop lay on the desk inviting a quick inspection. Unfortunately it was password protected. Paul hesitated for a moment then an idea came to him. At first he tried simplified combinations of numbers but nothing worked. Then trying to be more creative he considered words and phrases that had to do with drugs and illegal contraband, but again nothing happened.

Once again he tried and keyed in 'Hurricane Charley'—much to his chagrin, no entry.

He stood, frustrated. Disappointed that his efforts had failed, he moved back to the filing cabinet.

Immediately, the file heading 'HCharley' caught his attention, kindling a sudden epiphany. Moving back to the desk he typed in the word 'HCharley' as it appeared on the file heading. Bingo, the desktop appeared and he was in.

Elated, Paul searched the main documents file for anything that would point toward the drug operation but there was nothing other than legitimate, work related topics. He went back to the main menu and noticed the name 'Barry' at the top. Clicking on the name brought up several new documents.

The first document was the B.C. government-approved registration of a limited company in the name of H.C. Bathroom Products. This is what Paul had been looking for.

There were several other official documents with the company name and periodic renewal of directors which drew Paul's attention.

The forming of the company had taken place eight years previously, under three names: D.G. Homes, V. R. Groves, and B.T. Rushmore.

Paul whistled softly as he turned the names over in his mind. These people currently held high office in the community.

He clicked on a document labeled Accounts. Three multi-digit numbers were listed beneath the heading, each preceded by a letter. The letter preceding each of the numbers corresponded to the first letter of each director's last name.

Here was the evidence to build Paul's case— shared income from the proceeds of Hurricane Charley. Another document with meeting agendas showed the directors met once every two weeks, at a specific venue, to discuss business.

He quickly googled the address and it appeared to be an old warehouse not in regular use. Further research revealed the owner of the warehouse to be D.G. Homes.

He pulled a memory stick from his pocket quickly downloaded the file. He needed more evidence though, if he was going to make it all stick.

A quick investigation in a closet produced an unsealed box he immediately recognized. The box was labeled Bath Salts and a duplicate of the boxes he had seen in the rainforest laboratory, before the earthquake.

On Rushmore's desk was a framed family photograph, showing Rushmore striking a pose with a woman who was probably his wife. This gave Paul an idea.

He removed the box of Hurricane Charley from the closet and placed it next to the photograph on the desk. For good measure he placed a bottle of the box's contents on the other side of the photograph. Then, took a snapshot of the desktop setup with his cell phone camera.

Paul hurriedly replaced the box in the closet and pocketed the single bottle of the drug before calling it a day.

By the time he exited the study the whole escapade had taken only twenty minutes.

Dan was patiently standing on the ladder waiting for him to finish. They grinned at each other, packed up the ladder and left the house.

After Dan had dropped Paul at the family home, it was nearly lunch time. His suspicion involving the prominent names on the company registration documents still had had to be substantiated.

He called Angeline to see if she would be up to doing some research for him. The News Media resource archives might hold relevant information as to their public lives.

Although she had been told to take two weeks leave, Angeline readily agreed and said she would go into the news office and start the research immediately—she would try to have something available the following morning.

Paul gathered the family together for an afternoon visit to the hospital. When they entered, Paul was concerned that the privacy curtain had been drawn closed. No nurses were present so he peeked beyond the curtain and saw his wife sitting up, a bandage wound tightly around her head.

He was overjoyed to see she had at last woken up. Meg looked pale but she smiled when she spied his face. He quickly beckoned for Lillian and Jason to enter. A tearful family reunion took place after which Paul told his wife some of the detail regarding past events, since the earthquake. He did not mention that Amy was Rushmore's prisoner nor

269

that the family was in danger. He agreed with his mother that Meg, when she finally woke, should be given time before being told all the details; details of which Lillian, herself, had scant knowledge. Paul had promised to make a full disclosure of the status quo when he was ready.

**

Monday, 2nd October.

Angeline had spent most of her Sunday afternoon doing the vital research Paul had asked for. There had been several public appearances by two of H.C. Bathroom Products directors, Dennis Homes, chief of Victoria's police force and Victor Groves, the Minister of Environment, Lands and Parks. Rushmore's station in life was not as high profile as his two buddies. Rushmore was an executive in the local Revenue Canada, Customs and Excise office.

Angeline discovered the two men, Homes and Groves, had attended almost one hundred events and functions of a political and social nature over the twelve years, preceding the more recent registration of their drug distribution company. On each occasion they had been photographed sitting together. The clincher for Paul was that twenty of the events had included Rushmore and there were several photographs of the three sitting together, chatting like long lost friends.

The next day, Monday, she called Paul with the good news and they decided to meet at a local coffee shop so he could check over her findings. They spent a few hours going through all the research. He had brought the memory stick with him and they viewed its information to see if there might be any other avenue Angeline could explore but she appeared to have found enough for them to make a water-tight case against the directors.

With this knowledge in mind, Paul decided to put the next phase of his plan into action on the following day. He then asked Angeline to make copies of all the photographs and snippets of news she had unearthed involving the three men. He sat at the computer to write brief notes—one to each of Hurricane Charley's directors and one to the Assistant Chief of Police, Alan McDonald. The notes to Homes and Groves read:

TUESDAY: 3rd OCTOBER,

MEET ME AT THE WAREHOUSE TONIGHT AT 7:00 P.M. SOMETHING THAT COULD THREATEN OUR JOINT BUSINESS HAS COME TO LIGHT. DO NOT CONTACT ME PRIOR TO THIS. IT'S URGENT. REGARDS, BARRY.

The note to Rushmore was exactly the same in content but signed, 'Dennis Groves'.

Paul knew the directors would be careful as to how they contacted each other regarding their illegal business, so he purposely chose to type the notes and have them delivered to each person by courier.

The Assistant Chief of Police would receive an entirely different and anonymous note pertaining to the fact that high profile, influential members of the community were involved in an illegal drug syndicate—that a deal would be taking place on a specified evening in an old warehouse.

The note stressed that details would be made available in a package, to the attention of the Assistant Chief of Police, delivered to the Victoria Central R.C.M.P. offices, thirty minutes before the meeting in the warehouse was to take place.

Paul did this to prevent the Assistant Chief of Police from searching for clues before the Hurricane Charley directors came together for the meeting.

The notes were duly sent by courier to make sure they would reach the respective people that day. Paul had asked Angeline to phone each director's secretary to ensure they were not away on business.

At five p.m., he called Dan and then drove to the old deserted warehouse where they pried open a window to gain entry.

The only room in regular use was a store room lined with empty boxes and old pallets, situated down a narrow hallway that led off the front entrance hall. There were three chairs and a table in the center of the open area.

The single overhead fluorescent shone directly onto the table, the boxes and stacked pallets cast deep shadows against the four walls of the room.

A parcel, containing the single bottle of Hurricane Charley taken from Rushmore's study closet, was placed on the table with a note attached to it.

Finally, the stage was set to Paul's satisfaction. "That should do it. Angeline will deliver the package to the police in precisely thirty minutes. I can't wait to see the look on Rushmore's face when he opens the package."

"Let's hope the police arrive promptly," Dan added. "It's possible Rushmore may be armed but I don't think he would do anything stupid. Do you think the police might search the whole warehouse? We certainly don't want them to find us here."

"I doubt they would do that," answered Paul. "They'll have their hands full arresting the suspects."

The minutes ticked by as the two men waited for the arrival of the directors. Despite the cool air, both men perspired freely, the anticipation mounting with every second that passed.

They were well concealed by the stacks of pallets and boxes. With the overhead light lacking sufficient illumination, they were confident their presence would not be known.

A few minutes later a door opened at the far end of the building and a figure slipped into the warehouse. He was wearing a long, dark coat and a baseball cap. A cigarette dangled from his mouth as he looked furtively around, eyes focused on the table in the center of the warehouse floor.

Immediately following behind came another man —then Paul recognized the familiar figure of Rushmore. They walked slowly to the table, looking in all directions, unable to see the two figures hiding behind the pallets, stacked in the far corner.

Rushmore was clearly suspicious and he stepped up to the table, lifting the small parcel with its attached note. He said something to the other two and they stepped directly under the overhead light to examine the note, attached to the parcel.

It read:

TO BARRY, DENNIS, AND VICTOR. A LITTLE GIFT FOR MY THREE LOVERS. IT'S TIME YOU TRIED THE PRODUCT THAT HAS RUINED THE LIVES OF SO MANY PEOPLE. YOU HAVE RUINED MINE AND I AM ABOUT TO RUIN YOURS. HILDA RODGERS.

Rushmore looked at the other two men and they started laughing out aloud.

Rushmore said, "I told you guys, when we received those invitation notes that something like this was going to happen. We all know that Hilda is no longer around so it could only have been one other person. Fortunately I've prepared for this."

At that moment the door at the far end burst open and three uniformed men came walking in. The leader, a swarthy young R.C.M.P officer, greeted Rushmore and Homes in an obsequious manner, in turn shaking each hand.

Dan immediately recognized one of the men. It took him a few seconds to drag up the man's name from his memory—it had been some time ago. The officer was an old class mate from Victoria Secondary School, the school that Dan had attended soon after his arrival in Canada. Stephen Marks.

The leader asked, "Where is the person who sent the information to the assistant chief?"

Rushmore laughed. "Oh, I'm sure he's here somewhere—and Stephen, thanks for intercepting that package. Saved us a lot of headache."

The police officer smiled then looked around at the stacks of pallets lining the walls and called out, "Come out of your hiding place, Brinkworth! We know you're here!"

Paul felt a cold chill flow through his body. He glanced at Dan with a look of surprise and whispered, "How in the hell did they know about my plan?"

Dan looked as surprised as Paul and shook his head.

"Don't show yourself," whispered Paul. "They think I'm alone."

Dan nodded and Paul stepped out from the hiding place to face the group standing in the center of the room. He walked into the dim luminescence of the overhead light, his feelings awry. *How had Rushmore known?*

The R.C.M.P officer stepped forward and pulled out a pair of handcuffs. "Paul Brinkworth, I'm arresting you on suspicion of murder."

Paul was stunned. "Murder—what are you talking about? Whose murder?"

The officer responded, "The murder of Hilda Rogers and Andre Banville."

∞

Twenty

Incarcerated.
Tuesday, 11:00 a.m. 3rd October.

The guard shut the gate with a clang behind Paul as he was ushered into the interviewing room. After making the arrest the previous evening, the police had taken Paul to the Vancouver Island Regional Correction Center on Wilkinson Street, Victoria.

The law in British Columbia requires that if anyone is arrested and held for a period of up to twenty-four hours, a bail hearing must be sought with a local justice of the peace or a judge within that period.

The charging officer allowed Paul one phone call which he used to call his deceased father's lawyer and friend, James Coulson, the man who was waiting for him on the opposite side of the glass barrier in the interview facility.

Paul was relieved to see a friendly face after the two-hour interrogation he had endured at the hands of two police investigators, before being locked in a holding cell for the night.

Things could not get worse. It would appear that Rushmore and his friends had found a use for his services after all—he would now become the focus

277

of attention. The accusations Rushmore and his two cronies would have faced, had Paul and Angeline's package got through to its intended audience, would now be completely overshadowed.

The lawyer, picked up the black, plastic phone that served as an intercom between the two booths and waited for Paul to do the same.

"How're you doing, buddy?" Coulson asked.

"As well as can be expected under the circumstances," said Paul.

The lawyer continued. "I have reviewed the charges against you and it would appear that a notebook was found in the purse belonging to a Hilda Rogers, who you apparently had a meeting with on the day she was murdered."

"So they told me," said Paul with a scowl. "Hilda made a note of my name, the time and place—Ten Mile Point. I've actually never been to that area in my life. The evidence is totally false and obviously contrived."

"It had been reported to the police that you and a friend, Tom Wilson, had hard words with Miss Rogers and her colleague, while they were sightseeing in the rainforest near Tofino."

Paul divested himself of the whole story while the lawyer listened patiently, intently making notes on his notepad.

Finally the lawyer stood and said, "I will be in touch after I've spoken with your two friends, Dan and Angeline. Your accusers intend to bring the case before a judge later today, hoping that bail will not be granted but I don't see they have enough evidence to force that. I will be appearing in court on your behalf so cross your fingers."

The lawyer reset the phone and waved goodbye. Paul nodded, his face set in a grim expression of angst. He stood and indicated to the accompanying guard that the interview was at an end.

Later that afternoon the lawyer was back in the interviewing facility waiting for Paul to be brought from the cell. There was a frown on the lawyer's face as Paul shuffled into the booth and picked up the phone.

"Bail has not been granted, but we are working on it," said Coulson. "Don't worry—your two friends and I are putting together a stronger case for your release and I hope to be granted an injunction to change that decision."

**

Wednesday, 4th October.

It had been a week since the abduction. Night and day had passed with monotonous succession and the only reason she knew the time and date was by watching TV, a small flat-screen situated in one corner of the otherwise sparsely furnished room.

The TV service had resumed seventy-two hours after the earthquake and by watching the local news, it became evident that many towns on the island had suffered severe damage to buildings and roads.

Amy had spent many hours crying into her pillow. She did not want the guard, the woman who called herself Rose, to hear her pleas to God for her safety or her cries for her family. She missed them so much, even Jason, which was a definite first.

Rose had not spoken a word to her throughout the entire time of the incarceration. The entrance to the room had a door with an accompanying steel gate. The door remained open at all times but the gate was locked. Food was brought on a regular basis with a glass of water and the occasional cookie. At first Amy didn't eat anything. This was partly because she was in such a state of emotional distress, however on the second day of captivity, she became more demonstrative. When Rose opened the gate and placed a plate of foot at the bedside Amy grabbed it and threw it on the floor. The plate shattered and she glared at Rose defiantly. "You can't keep me here forever, you old witch! I'm going to starve myself to death unless you let me go."

Rose, keeping her composure, finally broke the ensuing silence. "Suit yourself. I'll bring some paper towels and you can clean this mess—or live with it, but I'll not put up with bad behavior."

This combination of emotional duress and hunger-strike behavior did not last long. Although Amy still felt a measure of emotional trauma, real hunger for food manifested on a continuous basis.

There seemed to be no end to her imprisonment. The shower and toilet were clean enough, with three bars of soap and several rolls of toilet paper stored beneath the sink.

She wondered about school—children had only been back to class for about three weeks, following the summer break, before the earthquake struck. They must be wondering where I am, she thought pensively.

She could see out the entrance, down the hallway, off which was a kitchen where Rose prepared her meals. Rose appeared to occupy a bedroom somewhere farther down the hallway.

The house had to be built into the side of a slope as there were no windows on the back wall of her prison, only a small, barred window high up the one side. Amy had tried to pry the steel bars off their mountings but without a knife or screwdriver it was an impossible task. Rose provided only plastic utensils with the food and always checked the window from the entrance when collecting the after-meal plate or bowl which Amy always left at the gate.

Late in the afternoon, Amy was watching CHECK-6 news on television, hoping to hear some news about her abduction. She thought it very strange that her father had not done anything to find her after a week. Dan, and the woman who was with them on that fateful morning, also appeared to have melted into obscurity; no one was even attempting to determine her whereabouts. Amy felt a terrible pang of rejection and longing for the life she once had.

Suddenly she was jolted out of her state of morass as the news anchor made a statement:

A Victoria man was arrested on suspicion of murder last night after police apprehended him in a deserted warehouse. The man, Paul Brinkworth, a seismologist working at the Geoscience Centre, is linked to the murder of two people and possibly a third...

Amy was stunned. This was not the news she had expected to hear. She threw herself on the ground and began screaming so loudly that Rose came running. "What is it, girl? What's wrong?"

All Amy could manage through her sobbing and tears was, "My father, my father..." and she pointed at the TV. Rose stood in silence and tried to listen to what the news anchor was saying.

Eventually she shook her head, gave Amy a sympathetic look and went back to the kitchen.

**

Thursday, 8:00p.m. 5th October.

Dan Duplessis, Angeline, and James Coulson, Paul's lawyer, sat around the living room table in Angeline's apartment, huddled over copies of the documents that had previously been sent to the R.C.M.P assistant chief, Alan MacDonald .

Dan picked up a photo of the three men central to their investigation and stared at it for the longest while.

He said absently, "There has to be someone who will believe our story. Someone who is not involved in this drug operation."

The lawyer frowned. "The three have made a statement to the police about Paul trying to frame them for drug trafficking—they want to include it as evidence that Paul was out to sink them because they knew he was guilty of killing Andre Banville."

"But Banville was alive when we left, barely, but alive," cried Angeline, with tears coursing down her cheeks. "Maybe O'Kelly killed him when he returned."

The lawyer looked thoughtful. "Paul did tell me exactly what happened and I have no doubt it's the truth, however, what a jury will believe is what really counts. We have to find proof."

Angeline dabbed at her eyes with a handkerchief. "How are we going to do that? The only other person we saw was the receptionist, who was not in her office when we arrived."

"I believe everything you say about this drug operation. I'm sure they will remove all trace of the laboratory in the rainforest and the destruction of the quake will largely cover their tracks. Paul said their outlet was located at the Woodgrove Mall in Nanaimo. They will also make sure there will be no trace of Hurricane Charley anywhere in that store," added the lawyer.

Angeline started to sob and Dan stood, went to her and placed his arm around her shoulder. "Don't cry, Angeline. We'll find a way out of this mess."

She immediately calmed and tried to compose herself. After a minute she looked glumly at the other two and said, "There's another problem. When I went back to check the records from where I took this information everything had been removed—every article and every photograph!"

"I guess we could expect that to happen," said Dan.

"These people are extremely well connected and we are going to need a miracle to bring a cast-iron case against them," said the lawyer.

Dan tried to stay in a positive frame of mind. "We must keep trying—we'll find something. What has happened regarding Paul's family?"

The lawyer shifted uncomfortably in his chair. "They didn't take the news very well, as you might expect. With Megan still convalescing in hospital, we decided to keep the news from her at this time but Paul's son and mother know he has been charged with suspected murder."

Dan remembered they faced an even greater obstacle. "What about his daughter, Amy—Rushmore has her locked up somewhere. God knows what that psycho will do to her."

Angeline started to cry again, remembering the ordeal she had gone through at the hands of Rushmore. It was something she couldn't verbalize. All she could manage was, "The man is not only a psychopath but also a sadist and should be hanged."

Dan walked to the kitchen counter and poured another cup of coffee. "What happens now?"

"Paul's bail hearing is set for the ninth of October—it will be not guilty, of course, but we really need to come up with something concrete before that. Hilda Rogers was murdered on the afternoon of Wednesday, September twenty-seventh, as far as the coroner could tell. Her body was found four days later."

The lawyer paused for a moment before continuing, "Paul visited the hospital on that day but no one can actually verify how long he remained at the bedside because the privacy curtains were drawn around Meg's bed—Paul's mother and son left at about three and caught a bus home, leaving him with the car."

"So...he has no alibi for about two hours that afternoon. Did no one see him leave the hospital?" asked Angeline.

"No—the nursing staff was extremely busy and nobody will say for certain they saw Paul leave. Unfortunately, two hours would give him enough time to drive to Ten Mile Point and then get home by just after 5:00 p.m."

"And how do they tie Hilda's murder to Paul," asked Dan.

"The police say they found a notebook in her purse which had a notation about a meeting with Paul at the murder scene."

Again the lawyer tried to add a positive note. "It certainly doesn't look good for Paul at this stage, but we must hope something comes up. Maybe one of the perpetrators made a mistake somewhere, at some time—all we have to do is find it."

*

Paul sat on the cell bed, cradling his head in both hands. How quickly things had changed for him, and for the worse. His mind was in a whirl and his emotions stretched to the limit. There was nothing he could think to provide more proof of his innocence in the light of the false evidence.

He thought of his wife and children, who would have to live without support through the many months he might be in prison—and if convicted, the many years of potential incarceration.

One thing he knew for sure: his family and friends would stand by him until he was proven innocent. It was however, a certainty he would lose his job, leaving the family with no financial backing.

He told the truth to the two police detectives who interrogated him. They had listened with little enthusiasm. When he told them about O'Kelly pursuing him through the mountains and the shooting of Tom Wilson, they had taken careful note but when they read the details of his statement back to him it all sounded so unreal. They raised their eyebrows when he mentioned O'Kelly shot Tom Wilson.

The interrogator added a side note that there was no evidence of a Sean O'Kelly and that Wilson's death seemed suspicious. When Paul accused Rushmore of trying to murder him and Angeline, ending with the dramatic rescue by Dan Duplessis, they did not believe such a rescue was possible. They said Dan would be interviewed but he might also become a person of interest. Rushmore had a cast-iron alibi for the period of time Paul was referring to as the day of the attempted murder.

They asked if he or Angeline could prove that Rushmore had actually raped her. Paul was unsure if Angeline would talk about it. He knew that with the time elapsed, there would be little, if any evidence of it.

Paul started to silently weep, his shoulders heaving with every sob. All the strain of the ordeal, the danger to his family, had taken its toll. His thoughts were running rampant: what about Amy? What would happen to her? The noose of fear was slowly tightening around his neck.

∞

Twenty One

Dan Plans a Course of Action.
Early Friday morning, 6th October.

The air was cool and the ground frosty as Dan walked through the nearby neighborhood park with Sultan following behind. The shepherd stopped every now and then to sniff out grassy areas and the bases of trees that lined the pathway, enjoying all the new smells that came to him. Dan needed time to clear his head after the events of the past week and a walk in the park was the best place for it. All the beautiful colors of the falling leaves decorating the lawns, brought that autumn feeling of change, the season Dan so dearly loved.

He thought about that night in the warehouse, when Paul had been arrested. Seeing an old school buddy, Stephen Marks, one of the arresting trio of police officers had him intrigued. There had to be something that he could do to turn the tables on Rushmore and his fellow criminals—Stephen may just be the key.

If the chief of police was involved, there would more than likely be a downward infestation of the rank and file also in on the deal, but it was worth looking into. He remembered Stephen as always

289

being someone easily led and invariably in trouble with authority. The R.C.M.P seemed a very unlikely vocation for him, unless he had changed considerably, which might not be out of the question.

Dan had decided to take a week's leave from his job in order to fix the small amount of damage his home had sustained during the quake. It would also be useful time to spend helping Paul out of the seemingly impossible position the seismologist found himself in. Other than James Coulson, Paul's lawyer, there was no one he could think of who was available or in a position to help. Dan liked Paul. They had become good friends in a short space of time, the fires of affliction having forged their relationship and consequent bonding. Something had to be done.

Sultan nudged Dan's leg with his snout, as if to say, *I know what you're thinking—just don't exclude me.* Dan reached down and ruffled the dog's ears. He knew what he had to do and turned for home with Sultan excitedly following at his heels.

Dan went on to Facebook and did a search for Stephen Marks. The name came up under the "friends, who are friends of the people you know" section and he quickly asked to be invited as a 'friend.' Then he did an internet search on the name and found interesting information on a family website that had been put up by Stephen's brother.

It appeared that Stephen and his brother were involved with a group called 'Philadelphia Brotherhood' but nothing was said regarding its purpose or activities.

Dan googled the name and Philadelphia Brotherhood had a website containing a blog on the building of muscle cars and hotrods. The front page featured very sexy women, scantly clothed, draped over the hoods of several of the brightly painted vehicles plus heavily tattooed dudes hanging around gawking.

Skimming the other search results, he was shocked to find an old article stating the group had been under investigation for trading in explicit photographs that might be considered pornographic but the case had been dismissed for lack of evidence.

The pages following contained some of the explicit photographs mentioned in the article. He agreed these portraits were pornographic, maybe even a little steamier than Playboy magazine. If Stephen was mixed up in this type of company, the image didn't quite fit with his involvement in the R.C.M.P.— something definitely did not meet the eye.

The afternoon was spent working on the house while Sultan slept on his mattress in the kitchen. Later, when the sun had gone down, Dan returned to his computer and immediately went to his

Facebook page. The invitation sent, to be a FB friend, had been approved by Stephen Marks and he noticed several photos of hotrods Stephen had posted, underscored by the remarks of his associates. Dan took the names of several people who made the comments and did systematic searches on each. They all had one thing in common: The Philadelphia Brotherhood.

A meeting of the Brotherhood had been planned for Saturday evening, 7th October, at their premises in downtown Victoria. They called it a social gathering 'by invitation only.' Dan knew of the building, a showroom for a well-known line of luxury sports and specialty cars, many featured on the website. At the back of the building was an auto-body shop used in the refurbishing of previous century vehicles which ultimately were transformed into the specialty versions.

An idea formed in Dan's mind; an idea so outrageous that he immediately discounted it, but then he thought—why not?

The next afternoon he left Sultan at home and drove to the Brotherhood's place of business. The sales and service section sold items such as caps and clothing to the general public. There were several people congregated in the store looking to make purchases, so Dan busied himself, picking out a cap that advertised the name of a sports vehicle. After a while he sauntered out toward the back of the property and found the door that led to the auto-body repair section. It was closed and there didn't appear to be any refurbishing taking place. He walked over to several old vehicles parked against the back wall and tried some of the doors until he found one open.

Slipping into the backseat he would wait until darkness settled on the city, hoping he had picked the right spot for his observations. At seven p.m., a vehicle pulled up and parked outside the auto-body shop. Three muscular dudes with skull and cross-bone tattoos got out and went to the door. There was an overhead light above the entrance so the men were visible in some detail. They unlocked the door and shuffled inside, leaving it open. Lights were turned on in the building, casting shadows across the backyard area.

Another car pulled up and spilled its occupants onto the pavement, all laughing raucously at some joke and carrying bottles of what appeared to be alcohol. A minute later a pickup parked adjacent to the main building and two men got out. They walked toward the back, to the open door and as they passed under the overhead light, Dan saw Stephen Marks. He too was carrying bottles of alcohol and passed quickly through the entrance to the interior of the building.

Dan was about to leave his hiding place when a forth vehicle appeared. He froze as he recognized the man who opened the door to the vehicle and stepped out—Rushmore. He held the vehicle's door open and four young children got out from the backseat. Dan's mind was in a whirl. What were children so young, doing at the Brotherhood's meeting. There were two girls and two boys, all seemed a little intimidated by Rushmore, who shoved them toward the open door of the auto-body shop.

Dan knew it could only be one thing and while he was terrified for the children he was also elated by the fact he stumbled onto something that could be the drug cartel's undoing—something so heinous, it defied the imagination.

**

Saturday, 9:00 a.m. 7th October.

Many days had passed in which the man suffered tremendous pain, however a driving force in him had helped to divert the agony into a more tolerable state—that of rage and hatred.

He would get through the inconvenience and pain because there was a score to settle. The bandages were changed twice daily. On the eighth day, they were removed altogether and for the first time he was able to see what the plastic surgeon had done for him.

At his request the nurse brought a mirror and when she had gone, he plucked up the courage to look at himself. There was little to comfort him. What was once his face was now a mass of healing skin that did not remotely resemble his original features. Hideous was not the word—perhaps monster was a better analogy.

The eyebrows were completely missing, plus a good deal of hair had been burned away. The two holes that served as eye sockets were so swollen that mere slits remained for his vision. What had once been pencil-thin lips were now thick balloons of flesh and new skin, taken from another part of his anatomy, had been pulled tightly over his cheekbones. Time would bring the swelling down. He could no longer look at the pitiful reflection, so he closed his eyes and cursed. A determination welled up within him to regain his strength and get out of the hospital as quickly as possible.

Two days later he was advised that several more operations would be required before the final product could emerge. Driven by his desire for revenge he determined the time had come for him to leave.

Early in the morning, on the tenth day of his recuperation, the man painfully rose from the bed and searched the lockers of the other patients in the ward while they slept. Soon he found what he was looking for—clothes that fit. Then he shuffled out of

295

the ward, walked through the reception area and left the hospital.

**

Monday, 11:00 a.m. 9th October.

James Coulson arrived at the correctional center and waited for the guard to usher Paul into the reception area.

"How are you are doing, buddy?" asked the lawyer with concern.

"It's tough," Paul said.

"I want to brief you for this morning's arraignment in court. With a judge already having refused bail at my first meeting I will make another attempt at getting that set up. Your wife has given me permission to use the value of the house if bail is granted."

"How is Meg holding up?" asked Paul, rubbing his red-rimmed eyes.

"The doctor will be authorizing her release from the hospital tomorrow. Of course, I had to tell her everything that has happened so far and she was understandably a little shattered. Your mother has been a great help and comfort to her. As per your instructions I have not told her about your daughter."

Paul shot Coulson a quick glance. "Will she be fit enough to come and see me?"

The lawyer looked doubtful. "I know she is desperate to see you but the doctor is being very protective of her. We will have to see—it's a matter of time."

"So, what will they decide in court this morning?" Paul wasn't sure if he really cared to know but asked anyway.

"The judge will read the charges against you and we will enter a plea of not guilty. I will try to get the previous bail refusal reversed but I'm not confident the new judge will concede to it."

Paul steeled himself to open his eyes and looked at the lawyer. "I really need to get out of this hole."

"I will do my best. You know that," the lawyer answered with conviction. "It's going to be a busy day for me. After the arraignment I have a meeting with Dan. He says he has some news and he believes it to be very good, so I am eager to hear what he has to say."

"Dan's a good man. At least that sounds a bit hopeful," said Paul, perking up a bit.

"You ready, buddy?"

Paul nodded.

"See you in the courtroom," the lawyer said as he replaced the intercom on its cradle.

At eleven a.m., Paul sat next to the lawyer waiting for the judge to enter. He still wore the orange colored coveralls the prison provided for their inmates. Sitting near the back, on their side of the room, was Dan, Angeline, and her boss, Andrew Mortimer. Behind them, alone, sat the director of the Geoscience Centre. The judge entered and everyone stoop up.

The proceedings did not take long, just as the lawyer had predicted. After the plea had been entered, Paul looked briefly at his friends who smiled and gave him a thumbs up. As predicted, bail was refused for the second time and Paul was led to the waiting shuttle.

When he had left the building, Coulson met briefly with Dan and Angeline in the court foyer. Dan was shaking with excitement and couldn't wait to talk about his discovery.

**

Monday, 11:25 a.m. 9th October.

Lisa Rushmore was having a difficult time with her daughter. The girl, a teenager, spent a great deal of time in her room and Barry, as stepfather, had refused to exercise any parental restrictions, giving young Heather carte blanche on anything the internet offered.

The girl was sullen and withdrawn, a law unto herself and had become increasingly uncommunicative—was it a teenage stage or were there deeper problems? Lisa was not sure.

Her marriage to Barry Rushmore, three years previously, had started well but then Lisa had, on two occasions, found lipstick on the collar of a shirt and when Rushmore had been confronted there had been an angry scene in which he threatened to walk out, saying she was paranoid and the lipstick had been an accident.

After time passed things appeared to improve between them but she noticed Barry had taken an unusual interest in Heather, whose figure was filling out into the image of a beautiful young woman. Remembering the previous confrontation, Lisa resisted any negative thoughts, trying to give her husband the benefit of the doubt. It remained, however in the back of her mind, like a dripping tap.

A short time after returning from Vancouver, having attended the national quilt festival and then her ill mother's bedside for a week, Lisa found a condom wrapper in the trashcan while she was emptying the garbage into a plastic bag for removal. She suspected the worst. Barry and Heather had spent a week in the Victoria home alone with each other—her mind churned unmercifully but she kept quiet, terrified of her husband's temper.

Finally, she could not retain her peace any longer and confronted her daughter on the matter.

Heather burst into tears and locked herself in the bedroom. Lisa did not know what to make of her daughter's behavior but took it as a sign of guilt.

Later that morning, her mind still stewing over the problem, Lisa went into the garage to look for a fat quarter of material she needed for a quilting project. She was rummaging through several boxes of old cloth when her eye caught a burlap sack behind the stack of boxes.

*

The late afternoon sun was gently sinking below the horizon, taking the final dregs of warmth with it. Dan sat in his pickup watching the house intently, hoping its occupant would leave, giving him the opportunity to do a quick search of the interior. He had never broken in on this basis before but his training as a DART member uniquely facilitated the option. He recalled how successful the search of Rushmore's house had been and it encouraged him that this particular home may yield the same dividends. Sultan sat on the passenger seat beside him, his head cocked to one side and eyes riveted on his master's face.

The home belonged to Stephen Marks, the R.C.M.P officer whom Dan suspected of having an involvement with Rushmore. Stephen's bio showed he had been divorced for two months and was living alone. His Facebook page was littered with responses to posts by the opposite sex, a typical flirtatious practice used by single males, hoping to lure a female into their domain.

Dan was not sure what the search would produce but he needed to find something that would link Rushmore to Stephen's outfit. The discussion with the lawyer in the courtroom foyer that morning had given Dan the momentum he needed to do what was necessary to provide evidence for the case against Paul and put an end to the Brotherhood. He would have to be careful. It was evident that a certain group of corrupt officers were involved in the protection of Rushmore. If it became known to them that their affairs were in danger of being exposed, they would close ranks.

Another ten minutes passed and eventually Stephen made his exit, leaving the house in semi-darkness with only the porch light on. Dan gave Sultan a command and the dog lay on the seat with his head between his paws. Dan crossed the road and quickly walked toward the back of the home, looking for any window that might have been left open. Part of the DART training had prepared him for dealing with the conventional house alarm, often a problem in the event of disasters. Being a police officer it was highly probable that Stephen would not even have an alarm for one of two reasons: divorces cost a lot of money, and sometimes police officers feel they are exempt from the run-of-the-mill crimes perpetrated against general society.

In either event, Dan was ready to deal with any scenario. He found what he was looking for—a window not latched, slightly cracked open for extra fresh air. He cut the window screen with his Swiss-army knife, leaving one side still attached to the frame and then gently opened the window.

The moment of truth was about to reveal itself. If a passive infrared picked up his movement he would have a very limited time for the search. From insurance company statistics he had gleaned that when a monitored alarm went off in a home it would take the alarm response unit an average of four minutes to be on the scene. If there was only an audible alarm, the neighbors would ignore it for at least ten minutes before taking some possible action.

Dan produced a flashlight from his pocket and searched for infrared passives but saw none. He breathed a sigh of relief. Stephen obviously felt he was exempt from general break-ins. He moved silently through the house until he identified a particular room as the office. One wall was lined with books on shelves and a desk was positioned against an adjacent wall. A laptop sat on the desk, connected to a printer and for a moment he toyed with the idea of taking the laptop with him, but it would make the break-in too obvious. There had to be something else. He checked the desk drawers and found only the top left to be locked.

There has to be a reason for that, he thought, removing the knife from his pocket. Sitting on his haunches he selected one of the special applications and wiggled it into the lock. It took a few minutes of delicate twists and turns before the lock popped open. A stack of files the only contents. The first file contained paper copies of utility bills, but the second, marked 'Philadelphia,' proved to have items of great interest.

∞

Twenty Two

Rushmore Takes a Trip.
Tuesday morning, 10th October.

The road construction crews had made great strides in clearing up the mess caused by landslides and rock falls that had hindered motorists traveling from Victoria to Nanaimo. It now took only two and a half hours to make the journey and Rushmore enjoyed the time spent driving, relishing the thought of what awaited him in Nanaimo—Brinkworth's pretty young daughter, Amy.

He had told his wife Lisa he would be away for the night. Everything was going according to plan: with the lab in the forest now moved to another location and the store outlet in Nanaimo cleaned out, there was nothing anyone would find to penetrate the strong fortress of the Hurricane Charley operation. There had been a delay in production but it was better to lose a bit of profit in lieu of possible exposure. Brinkworth would take the fall for the murders of Hilda Rogers and Andre Banville—and possibly that of Tom Wilson. Even

O'Kelly was gone from the scene and Rushmore felt extremely pleased with himself.

The thought of spending the night with young Amy excited him and he couldn't wait to get to Nanaimo. His Aunt Rose would be given the night off. He had a soft spot for Rose, the sister of his now deceased father. Rushmore had stepped in to help her financially when her husband had been killed in a work related accident. She didn't know everything about Rushmore's business but felt bound to the income his activities brought her. Her deceased husband's estate had provided very little financial support and at the age of sixty-two, there was little to no chance of her competing in the job market.

Rushmore whistled loudly as he traveled along, sure of his safe position within a society of people who were victims of their own greed. Homes, the chief of police was in his pocket and so was Groves, the Minister of the Environment. He had exploited their weaknesses and lined their pockets with wealth—they owed him. Life couldn't be better and he felt like a king in a domain of plebs.

It was lunchtime when he drove up to the front of the Nanaimo house. Rose greeted him at the door and they sat in the living room for a quick chat. There were four bedrooms on the top floor of the house. Two were used as storerooms for legitimate bathroom products and one specifically for Hurricane Charley. The fourth bedroom was Gus's, the manager of the Woodgrove outlet store. Rose stayed in the basement area and did the inventory bookkeeping for the island stores. They had other outlets in Victoria, Courtenay, and Campbell River, all thriving island-cities and several on the mainland that had a similar setup as the Nanaimo operation.

Rose served lunch and they ate the meal together, chatting about the various aspects of the inventory.

Rose was curious. "You didn't tell me why this young girl is a prisoner—what has she done?"

Rushmore was silent for a few moments before answering, "She represents a danger to our enterprise; at least her father does."

"What sort of danger?" she asked, with a fork full of food poised in front of her mouth.

Rushmore became irritated. He considered his aunt to be more of a hired hand than a family member and he didn't like anyone asking too many questions. "Real danger, Rose. Enough for me to keep her until the threat goes away."

Rose was taken aback by his attitude. "I've asked Gus to buy her some clothes—poor girl has nothing to wear and she's getting bored. I just want to know how long she'll be with us."

Rushmore considered the question. "Not too long now. I'll be staying the night and that will alleviate her boredom, I can assure you."

Rose gave him a stern look. "You're not thinking of..."

"I'm not going to hurt her—just help her understand what life is really about," he said with a grin. "You take the night off."

Rose contemplated her nephew's response and decided not to ask any more questions as the intent was clear. She had never considered him as one who had a thing for young girls.

"Okay," she said in resignation. "I need to get out anyway, so it's just as well."

She busied herself clearing the dishes, depositing them into the dishwasher. Rushmore stood at the kitchen entrance and said, "I will be back around six tonight. Leave the girl in her room—she can't escape."

Rose nodded and went about setting up the dishwasher.

Later that evening, sometime after six p.m., Rushmore returned to the house. He was feeling the effects of downing two vodkas at the White Spot, a popular restaurant on the mall premises, something he often indulged in when anticipating the company of the opposite sex. His sexual libido was heightened by the thought of introducing a young girl to the art of making love. His own step-daughter, Heather, had been among the first of many and thinking of that act brought his senses

307

into a frenzy. He took the steps three at a time and went straight down to Amy's basement prison.

**

Tuesday, 3:00 p.m. 10th October.

The lawyer inspected the photographs with disgust. Gradually the look of repugnance faded and a glimmer of a smile played around his lips as he sifted through a dozen pictures. Dan and Angeline sat impassively opposite him at the table, waiting for his comments. "It would appear your old pal, Stephen, doesn't trust digital images," he said finally.

Dan and Angeline both raised their eyebrows and waited for him to elaborate.

The lawyer looked up at them and continued. "Digital photos are always stored on a computer. Its common practice now among people who perpetrate this type of crime: they don't trust the internet because there are so many checks and balances so they trade in real photos. These particular pictures were probably being kept by Officer Marks for his own occasional perusal."

Dan smiled and added, "That makes perfect sense, I suppose. They are very explicit and confirm what I saw at the Philadelphia Brotherhood's meeting place Saturday night."

Angeline leaned forward. "The photos also tie Rushmore and the Police Chief, Dennis Homes, directly to the Brotherhood and their pornographic ring." She picked up two of the photos and perused them. They contained images of Rushmore and the police chief in very explicit and obvious acts of pornography.

"Stephen must have taken these without their knowledge and kept them as insurance, or something like that," said Dan.

"Those poor children, some of them are only about five years old. We are dealing with some very sick minds here," said the lawyer.

"What do we do now—surely we have the evidence we need to sink Rushmore?" asked Dan.

The lawyer leaned back in his chair. "We have enough to have him linked to a child sex scandal but not enough to clear Paul of the murder charges."

Dan was about to argue the point when the lawyer's cell phone rang. It was his personal secretary. He listened for a few seconds and then ended the call.

He looked at them and motioned for them to wait while he made a quick call. Dan and Angeline sat in silence as they listened.

The lawyer dialed the number and waited for the response. "Mrs. Rushmore? Thank you for calling my office—you have something you want to share with me?"

The lawyer listened patiently and in conclusion to the conversation said, "Thank you so much, Mrs. Rushmore; hold onto your discovery. I will be there in about fifteen minutes," then he ended the call.

Dan and Angeline were sitting on the edge of their seats in anticipation of what sounded like good news.

"We're in business," said the lawyer, finally.

*

The lawyer left Angeline's apartment, taking with him all the gathered evidence and drove to the police headquarters. On arrival he asked for Alan MacDonald, and was told to wait in the reception. A minute later the assistant chief of police appeared, beckoning for him to follow and they walked down the hallway to an office.

The assistant chief beckoned for Coulson to sit before taking his own seat behind a large oak desk. He looked at the lawyer enquiringly. "You have something for me?"

The lawyer lifted his briefcase and placed it on his lap. "I believe I have the evidence you require in order to expose the problem we face."

MacDonald raised his eyebrows. "Let's have a look."

After viewing the photographs the deputy chief responded. "This is enough to put Homes and

Rushmore away for some time but I don't see any connection to the murders that Brinkworth is charged with."

The lawyer smiled. "For that I will need you to accompany me to Rushmore's home. His wife, Lisa, has a very interesting story to tell us, plus, what I believe to be evidence that Rushmore murdered Hilda Rogers."

Once again, the lawyer's phone jangled noisily in his coat pocket. He quickly motioned to the assistant chief that he needed to take the call. When he had finished he said, "Things are getting better and better. That was Brinkworth's mother. Some woman has just dropped her granddaughter, Amy, off at home. It would appear the story of Amy's abduction by Rushmore is true. If you act quickly you will find a house in Nanaimo that ties Rushmore to the drug cartel I previously told you about. "

MacDonald picked up his phone and called the Nanaimo branch of the R.C.M.P. When he had finished talking to the Nanaimo police chief he replaced the phone and said, "You are quite correct—this day is becoming more interesting with each minute. Let's visit Mrs. Rushmore."

**

Thursday, 12:00 p.m. 12th October.

The nights had been long and cold. The prison cell smelled of stale smoke and urine, the seal on the small toilet in the corner being slightly dried out, allowing an occasional drip onto the floor.

Paul woke slowly and surveyed the starkness of his domain. It had been sixteen days since his incarceration and he had all but lost hope that any solution would be found to his present predicament.

Many conflicting thoughts crowded his mind, making it difficult to maintain any single train of thought that might lead to his defense in the trial that would surely come.

His adversaries had obviously planned their whole strategy and dealt with any possible contradictions to their case against him. The lawyer, James Coulson, had last been in to visit over ten days ago.

All visitors, other than legal counsel had been barred from seeing him and the strain of being away from his family had begun to take its toll.

Coulson had brought notes from both Dan and Angeline, who tried to assure him he was not forgotten and they were doing everything in their power to secure his release. So far there appeared to be very little working in his favor.

The hours passed slowly. He had asked one of the guards to bring him some reading material and an hour later was given several old magazines, however, he could not really focus on any of the articles.

News of the outside world was scant—the inmates only being herded into a courtyard for exercise one hour each day, knew nothing. Newspapers were not allowed, so nobody could find out anything about the state of the earthquake ravished city or what systems were back on line. All Paul knew was they had running water and electricity. The food was of a substandard quality but, never-the-less, edible.

The guard stopped at his cell. "Someone to see you, Brinkworth. Come with me."

Paul jumped off his bed and followed the guard along the corridor toward the interview room. The guard kept walking and when Paul hesitated at the entrance gate to the interview facility, he was told, "Keep moving, Brinkworth—your visitor is waiting."

Paul moved forward and wondered what lay in store for him. They passed through two more gated sections before they reached the general reception area where he saw the familiar figure of Coulson waiting for him. The lawyer was wearing a broad smile and shook Paul's hand as they met together.

"Let's get your things, buddy—you're free to leave."

"What?" Paul asked incredulously. "I'm free? What are you talking about—is this some sort of joke?"

"No joke, bud. Let's get your few belongings and I'll explain everything."

Paul followed the lawyer to a counter where a correctional center employee retrieved a tray containing his clothes, shoes, wristwatch, and wallet.

In a daze he signed a piece of paper on a clipboard and then followed the lawyer through the front entrance and to the car park. Coulson did not say another word until they were seated in his BMW and zooming toward the entrance gates of the center.

Paul looked across at the lawyer in amazement. "I have to be dreaming—tell me I don't have to wake up and find myself back in that cell?"

"You're not dreaming, buddy. This is real. So, let me explain the most recent happenings. New evidence was brought against your accusers from unexpected sources."

Coulson was ecstatic. "Rushmore's wife, Lisa, provided the police with new evidence that you did not murder Hilda Rogers. She had read of your incarceration in the Victoria Herald and fortunately

314

did not go directly to the police with her findings—
she came straight to me."

The lawyer went on to explain that Lisa
Rushmore had found a blood soaked towel hidden
in her garage while looking for cloth for a quilting
project. She knew of her husband's association with
Hilda Rogers and had often suspected he was seeing
her. When Hilda Rogers's murder appeared in the
news she wondered if her husband had something
to do with it.

"She also recently found out her fourteen year
old daughter and Rushmore were having a sexual
relationship. This further embittered her against
him, enough to tie him to the blood-soaked towel
and turn him in. DNA on the towel matched that of
Hilda Rogers."

Paul listened enthralled and could hardly believe
his ears.

The lawyer turned toward Paul and grinned. "The
best news of all is that your daughter, Amy, is safe.
She was being kept prisoner in a house up at
Nanaimo. This house was also a storage area for
Hurricane Charley. Apparently on Tuesday,
Rushmore arrived at the house which is looked after
by an elderly woman. It would appear this woman
worked for Rushmore and was also looking after
Amy. Amy doesn't really know what transpired
between this woman and Rushmore, but that

afternoon after Rushmore had left, the woman came to Amy and set her free."

"She set Amy free?" asked Paul, amazed at his change of fortune.

Coulson couldn't help laughing at the look on Paul's face. "All the woman said to Amy was that she couldn't take anymore of Rushmore's attitude. She said Rushmore wasn't getting the opportunity to ruin your daughter's life, too."

"What do you mean?" asked Paul uncertainly.

"Apart from pedaling drugs, Rushmore is involved in a pornographic child sex-ring called the Philadelphia Brotherhood—you can thank your pal, Dan, for coming up with that evidence. My guess is he came for Amy that day but the woman, bless her soul, had become attached to the girl and wasn't going to allow Rushmore to abuse her."

Paul closed his eyes and offered up a silent prayer of thanks.

The lawyer was not finished. "The deputy police chief, Alan MacDonald, and I produced the evidence together to the same judge who arraigned you and we were granted an injunction to have bail granted until all the evidence is officially verified."

Paul did not say a word. He was completely dumbfounded but gratified that Amy was safe and he was free to go home to his family.

Coulson continued. "It seems that Dennis Groves, the current police chief, is being investigated for tampering with evidence and several other indiscretions involving his high office. Dan's old school chum, Stephen Marks is in prison, plus several members of the Philadelphia Brotherhood and they will be brought to trial soon."

For the first time in a week Paul had something to smile about. "I want to go home," is all he could say.

∞

Twenty Three

Back to Work.
Wednesday, 9:05 a.m. 18th October.

Paul sat at his desk reading the newspaper. Things were slowly returning to normal at the Geological Survey Centre. John Fowler had advised the director he was regretfully resigning his position due to his wife's insistence they move to a safer part of the world and had immediately been let go.

The director had been fully informed of all that had transpired regarding Paul's incarceration and his consequent exoneration. He had wanted Paul to take well-deserved leave, but the seismologist was insistent it would be better for him to stay and bring order to the division. Paul felt he needed to orient himself with his new post as head of the Earthquake Studies division.

Paul's wife, Meg, was recuperating well, having arrived home to the joy of her family. The charge against Paul for the murder of Hilda Rogers had been dropped. The charges for the murders of Andre Banville and Tom Wilson were also dropped for lack of evidence.

The newspapers were full of the recent drug syndicate and child-sex ring bust that the R.C.M.P.

had made. There was a long article about the three directors of the H.C. Bath Products Company who had abused their positions to further their need for wealth.

It also mentioned that a local seismologist had been framed by these men for the murder of Hilda Rogers but new evidence had placed the guilt on Barry Rushmore's shoulders.

Paul had visit Gertrude Wilson and spent an awkward hour with her, agonizing over the details of her husband's death. There remained just one more important issue to deal with—Angeline.

He had spent many hours thinking about his relationship with her and had finally arranged to meet her one afternoon to settle the matter. He was still experiencing a measure of conflict with his feelings, but he knew for once, his head had to prevail over his heart.

The meeting between Paul and Angeline was that afternoon and he glanced nervously at his wristwatch, preparing to keep a firm grip on his emotions.

At ten minutes to three he left the office and walked to the parking area, where a brand new Jeep awaited him. The Geological Centre had leased the vehicle for him in replacement of the old Jeep, which now rested at the bottom of the Northumberland Channel. His mind was preoccupied with the pending meeting and after leaving the grounds he did not notice a car pull out behind him.   The car followed to the coffee shop in Sidney where he and Angeline had arranged to meet.

After parking the Jeep, he strolled into the shop and found her waiting for him.   Paul kissed her lightly on the cheek, his heart beating like a base drum. She smelled delightful, like a beautiful flower garden in springtime.

Angeline looked longingly at him as he took her hand in his.

"How are you?" he asked.

"I'm good," she answered, looking deeply into his eyes.

While they talked, a man shuffled into the shop and sat at the table next to them. His general appearance was scruffy and his clothes were filthy. The peak of the man's baseball cap sat just above his eyes, casting a slight shadow over his face.   He gazed at Paul and Angeline with interest but they took no notice of him.

At that moment a waitress appeared and they ordered coffee.   After they had been served, Paul hesitantly came to the point.

"Angie, I want you to know that despite the trials and tragedies we've been through, I enjoyed every moment being with you. I know we both feel something for each other..." His voice trailed off as he fought for the relevant words to say.

She looked down at her hands and tears welled up in her eyes. "I know what you're trying to say and understand your dilemma. You have so many years of happy marriage behind you, and your wife and children desperately need you."

Paul fumbled in his pocket for a handkerchief and gently began to wipe the tears from her cheeks. There was a lump the size of a mountain in his throat and he couldn't trust his voice to say anything. She clenched his hand tightly and continued.

"I could never do such a thing to your family, but I want you to know I'll never forget you." She stood and looked down at him with tears coursing down her cheeks. "We must not meet again—it will be less painful that way."

The man at the table next to them stood and without warning pulled out a gun. He kept the gun low, on his thigh and angled it upward, aimed at Paul's chest.

"Finally, I have you both in the same goddamn place. We have a score to settle and this time you are not getting away."

Paul's mind flipped cartwheels trying to figure out what was going on—then it dawned. He looked at the badly disfigured face. The scar tissue made the man look like a scarecrow. The eyes, dark and set back in surgically fashioned sockets, revealed a journey of pain and suffering.

It was the voice that solved the mystery. "O'Kelly! I thought you were dead."

Paul could not mistake that Irish accent. Angeline sat down again and stared in disbelief.

O' Kelly kept the gun trained on Paul. He did not want to draw any attention—fortunately there were no other customers in the shop. His face could convey no emotion but his eyes flashed hatred.

"Let's get moving—outside, to your vehicle!" They got into the Jeep and O'Kelly ordered Paul to drive toward Schwartz Bay. Within minutes they were on Route 17, heading north. Paul was thinking furiously for a way to distract the Irishman, but O'Kelly was watching him like a hawk. They drove in silence.

Ahead was a pickup truck. In the back was a shepherd yapping happily at the wind. Paul's heart almost skipped a beat as he recognized Sultan.

Paul had to attract Dan's attention without alerting O'Kelly. Angeline had also seen Sultan and glanced at Paul in silent acknowledgment. They drew closer to the back of the pickup and Paul flicked his headlights several times using the only Morse code he remembered from his days as a boy scout—the dots and dashes of the SOS signal. He prayed O'Kelly had not noticed.

Angeline looked straight ahead, afraid to catch Paul's eye again in case o'Kelly noticed.

Dan, who was travelling up to Schwartz Bay to do some fishing, saw the driver of the vehicle behind flick the headlights several times, but before he could lift his hand in acknowledgment the vehicle behind swung out, narrowly missing the rear of the pickup and went by at speed. Dan recognized Paul and Angeline sitting in front and noticed a third person in the backseat. He remembered Paul telling him the GSC were going to get him a new vehicle but he had not yet seen it. The two seconds that it took for the vehicle to pass his pickup were revealing—Angeline had looked at him with fear written all over her face. Then he realized that Paul had given the SOS signal, using the vehicles headlights.

That's very odd. Something is definitely amiss here. He thought, dropping back a little.

*

Eventually O'Kelly spoke: "Turn off here at this gravel road."

Paul obeyed. He prayed that Dan would follow. The gravel road ended on the beach and he stopped the Jeep close to the water's edge. They got out and O'Kelly brandished the revolver in their faces.

"Well, as you can see, my life has changed a little since we last met. Look what you've achieved, Brinkworth. I will never be attractive to anyone again. No one has need of a fucking monster."

Paul cleared his throat. "You won't achieve anything by killing us, O'Kelly. Hasn't there been enough death and destruction?"

"Your deaths will fulfill the quota very nicely. You have ruined my life and there's nothing for me to look forward to. I would be an idiot by allowing you, or your girlfriend, off the hook."

Paul realized O'Kelly, driven by his rage, was no longer sane. There would be no stopping him.

*

Dan followed the Jeep down the gravel road. He knew where it led and quickly began to search for a place he could hide his vehicle from the view of the of the Jeep's occupants.

Several trees on the left caught his attention and he turned off the road, hoping he would not be too late. He sensed danger for Paul and Angeline.

Calling Sultan to heel he ran to where the road descended toward the beach. He saw the Jeep parked near the shore's edge—a chilling sight met his eyes.

A man with a gun had backed Paul and Angeline to the water line. They stood, forlornly looking around them.

The man was talking. Dan listened until he caught something of what was being said. He had only moments to save them. Without further thought he gave his dog an order.

"Attack, Sultan!"

The shepherd had been waiting in eager anticipation and shot forward in great leaps and bounds, his fierce eyes glinting in the late afternoon sun.

O'Kelly heard the noise behind him and swiveled awkwardly. Seeing the swiftly approaching animal only a few feet from him, he hastily took aim and fired. The bullet struck Sultan high on the shoulder, momentarily slowing his charge, but the momentum was enough to carry him to the Irishman.

Before O'Kelly could fire off another round, the dog was upon him, taking him to the ground.

The revolver flew into the air as the ninety pounds of dog straddled the flailing Irishman. Although injured, the dog did not shy from the task at hand and took O'Kelly by the throat.

Dan took seconds to cover the distance and called Sultan off. The Irishman lay on his back stunned, unable to move. The pain from his burn wounds flared like a raging fire—it started a flashback of the terrible accident that had almost taken his life.

This time it was not real, but his damaged mind made him believe the flames were once again consuming his body.

Paul held Angeline tightly in his arms. She was close to fainting.

He looked at Dan and said: "Now, I believe there must be a God."

∞

In Conclusion

Thursday, 10:00 a.m. 19th October.

The next morning, Paul and Angeline were sitting in the same coffee shop discussing all that had happened the previous day. She had requested they meet again to bring some finality to their relationship.

O'Kelly had been placed in police custody and charged with the murder of Tom Wilson and Andre Banville. Sultan's injury, according to a veterinary surgeon, would heal with time and no permanent damage had resulted.

Paul awkwardly broached the subject of their relationship. "Angie, I've been trying to analyze my feelings and I feel like a man trapped between two very strong forces—love and integrity."

Angeline framed her words carefully. "I don't want to be a burden to you, Paul. I wish you happiness and peace. My life will never be the same, but I'm sure, in time, I will get over my loss."

Paul felt his heart was going to break and he remained silent.

Angeline stood and smiled through the tears. "Bye, my love."

Without looking back she strode out of the shop and left him sitting, like a lost and lonely child.

Five minutes later Paul regained his composure and smiled. He strolled out to the new Jeep and a verse from the Bible came to his mind. A phrase that he remembered from his Sunday school days:

A time to weep and a time to laugh... to everything, there is a season.

When he thought of how close he had come to death during the preceding days, he gained a sudden glimmer of understanding: *Life is short and must be lived to the fullest—every day is a gift. I have a beautiful family and I love them very much.*

He had endured a time of danger, disaster, turmoil, and trial. He had witnessed one of the greatest natural phenomenon of the present age—lost a good friend and gained another—been accused of murder and lost a relationship that was beginning to mean a great deal to him—but he had survived.

Paul realized afresh, how much he had to be thankful for. Somehow, despite the carnage and loss, life had taken on new meaning. Natural disasters were temporary infractions that exposed the frailty of life. It was not for him to question the rhyme or the reason—only to be thankful he was alive.

It would be years before things returned to normal, but then what was normal? A new challenge had presented itself.

After all, he thought, *isn't that what life is all about—rising to meet the challenge?*

A month later it came to Paul's attention that Dan Duplessis and Angeline Summers had announced their engagement.

THE END

MORE BOOKS BY COLIN SETTERFIELD

The Helium-3 Conspiracy
Love Sweat Tears
* The A-Mortal Gene
* The Habitat Relocation Project
* The Beautiful Planet
** The Memory Hunter.
** Merlin's War
** The Omega File
** Operation Terra Firma

* Survival of a Species Trilogy
** Special Agent O'Malley FBI Series.

9 781988 719054